CROWN OF RUINED OATHS

AN EMPIRE OF CURSES AND DREAMS NOVEL

THE NIGHT AND RAIN SERIES
BOOK 1.5

SUSAN PERSON

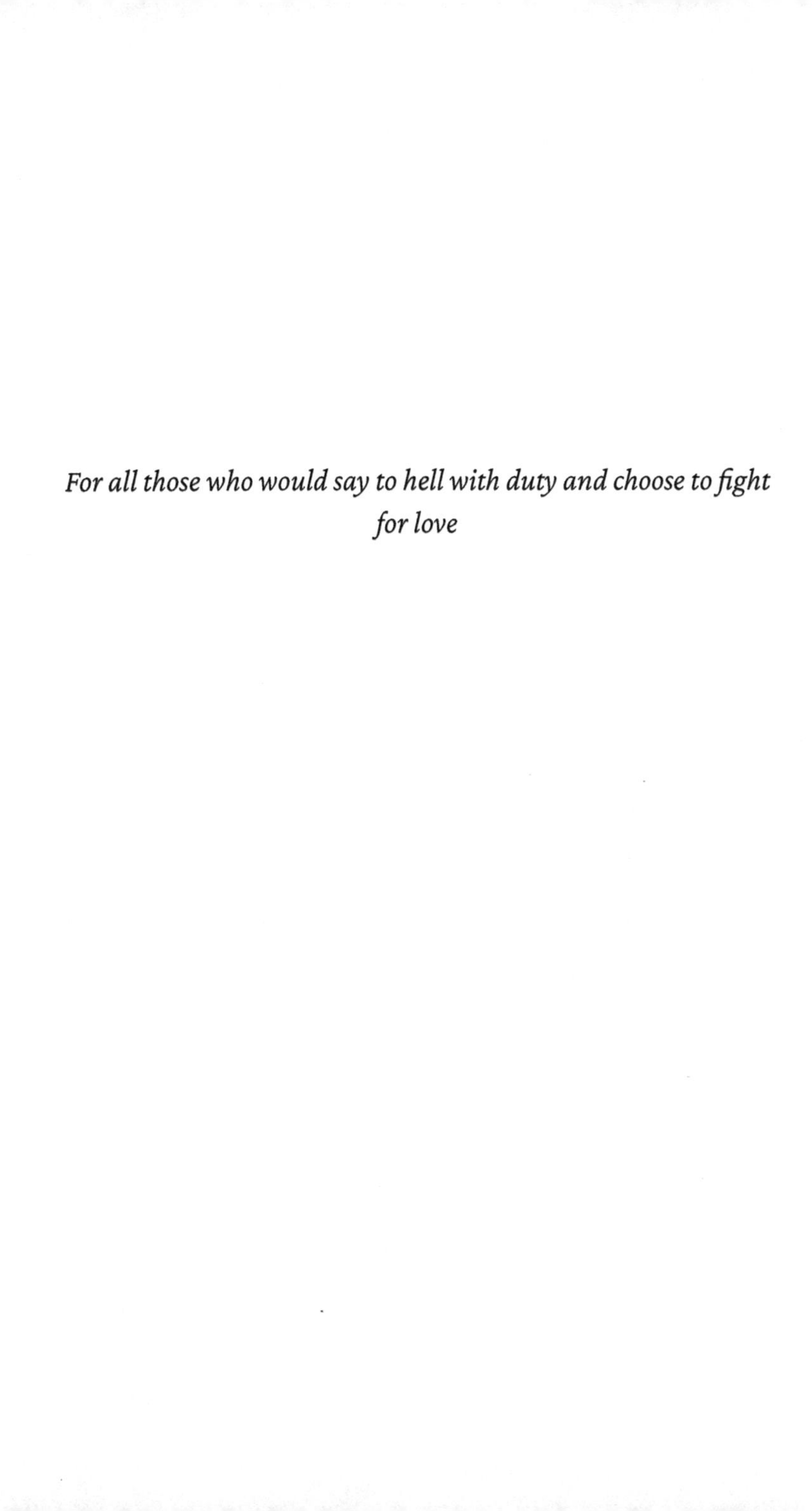

For all those who would say to hell with duty and choose to fight for love

Author's Note

Dear Reader - Please be advised that this book series contains content that may be upsetting for some readers. Should you wish to learn more information for your best reading experience, please scan the QR code below for additional details and content notes.

CONTENTS

CROWN OF RUINED OATHS

PART ONE
THE MOUNTAIN

From the Unicorn Archives passed down through the leaders to the historians.

Sprites and unicorns long lived in harmony, sharing knowledge and culture. Although both disagreed on which species claimed the honor of being the oldest, they maintained a close relationship on their shared lands.

As time passed, the sprites retreated to care for their own. Their kind died off in record numbers, never seen before in this realm. The oldest and most powerful came to the great unicorn leader to warn him of the battle to come. The sprites couldn't stay to fight but swore they would return with Nyx and Erebus.

Neala, the daughter of the sprite queen, gave of

the realm magic to the unicorn leader, telling him that one day fae children with unicorn power would be the ones to renew the realm. Sadly, she said, many of the unicorns and sprites would not live to see the day.

CHAPTER I
FOUR LEGS

Erebus, I'd made some mistakes in my three hundred *years, but this had to be the most colossal fuck up.* My bonded oath shredded because I fell in love. Perhaps the worst of my deeds, my charge, a princess in her own right, was left unguarded with her mate. The failure of my actions gnarled inside me like a rotting tree root. My hooves pounded the ground, skirting the farthest path outside the palace gate. I'd rarely been in my faelike form since I left Gemma and Laurel. There had been a time when it had felt as natural as my other, but that had been years ago. I checked in on my bonded and her family through my brother, Marius, but being on two legs brought too many memories. I dreaded each sunrise and every sunset, because it meant another day without Gemma. The wind blew the earthy scent around me, but all I could think of was her.

Gemma's face—the way light cascaded over her red

locks and across the small upturn of the end of her nose—made its rounds through my mind. Fae didn't freckle like humans, and her skin was a soft, milky cream with tiny specks of shimmer. I'd fallen in love with Gemma not long after our bonding ceremony when she was twenty. Something changed with us that day, and it wasn't the normal strengthening of the bond. I'd felt it in my soul, but I hadn't let myself admit it...not until she found her mate, Laurel. *A mate.*

I'd walked away, but I missed them both. Being away from them this long ached like a painful stabbing, like my heart had been pierced. In a superior unicorn way, I'd left them without a hint of a way to contact me, except through my twin. *Erebus, I am worse than an asshole. Since our assholes are likely the first part of us that forms in the fetal stage, I guess I'm reverting way back.*

Gemma and Laurel's fated status was too important to ignore. When I'd wanted to utter the word "mine" over and over again while the three of us made love, I convinced myself it was their mate connection coming down my bond with Gemma. Fewer fae found their mates since the war, much like how unicorns hadn't been able to reproduce since then. *Sort of.*

When the war ended, something had shifted and changed the world for all of us over the last two hundred years. Marius was our youngest leader in a millennium. Although I was technically the eldest of us, our father had put my brother in the line of succession ahead of me. I wasn't bitter about the decision. Not at all. I was relieved by the choice. When I asked my father why, he'd said, *because you are destined for something greater*. At the time, I thought he was blowing sprite dust up my ass, but I'd felt differently after my time with Gemma and Laurel as if a part of me had been asleep for centuries and had suddenly awakened—as if they had awakened it in me. Still, I couldn't touch that new piece of me, and inside, my heart seemed to search for theirs to beat together. I was convinced my brother knew more about what was happening to our world and me. Just as I was convinced Casimir was his chosen, despite how he tried to be a one-unicorn repopulation machine.

I ran full-out on all four legs, my head held high, scenting the air around me for others. Glorious joy spread through me as the soft green blades of the grassland brushed against my true form. Thank Erebus for this gift. The freedom overwhelmed my senses and wiped out my worries for a few moments. While it was easiest for me to move in the fae world glamoured as one of them, a unicorn was what I was meant to be. Another reason Gemma and I couldn't be together. What I hadn't expected out of everything that occurred after Gemma discovered the truth of the prison kingdom was to care for her mate with such intensity.

I'd come to love Laurel too. It was different from the deep vise Gemma had on me, probably because of our bond. The love I had for Laurel was light, fun, and care-free...and not mine to have. They were mates, and that was the end of that.

Their baby girl, who would share the similar gifts of Nyx as her aunt, Arianna, would be fine. Casimir had sent word to me that she would work with Marius to monitor the timing to extract Arianna. Too soon and they'd free Albert, Gemma and Arianna's father, from his far-too-pleasant prison. He deserved a death worse than any that could be dealt in this realm. General Daphina, the women's mother, was far too good for that prison. The fae king could have killed Albert and let Daphina go, but he said there had been enough bloodshed. He'd tasked the general with devising the prison, and she delivered. Many thought the king had already started going mad. The real truth lied in the archives with the museum curator, Whit.

When Albert's journals had been recovered after the Great War, they were immediately turned over. Whit kept them under a magical lock and key only he could open, and where no prying eyes could find them. He'd only shared them with my father, Marius, and me. I wasn't sure Gemma would forgive me for keeping the secret from her that Albert's biological father was King Veran, but I wasn't sure anyone needed to know that very fact sparked the Great War either. I'd broken my oath as a bonded, and breaking the oath to my father that we would never speak of Albert's journals seemed to cross a line I wouldn't be able to come back from. A familiar, colorful scent drifted to me.

Leana's mane flowed in the wind ahead of me. I slowed my pace and drank in the sight. She'd always been one of the most striking of our species, and I was sorry that she had been forced to partner with me. I didn't know why I was incapable of loving her. She exuded kindness along with strength in her convictions and never pressured me. Until I experienced the intimacy I had with Gemma, I'd thought I was unable to be impassioned. Awkwardness built a tight knot around my heart, but I was happy to see her. She'd been my friend long before we were paired.

The closer I got, I realized someone stood near Leana. A little fae. Drew, Gemma's little brother, danced around in front of her. He smiled and spun until he was dizzy. His laughter carried on the wind as he staggered off balance after so many spins. He'd grown a lot, but it had been years since I'd seen him. His once light-colored hair was tinted a golden brown. I'd expected her to declare him her charge, but she hadn't. What was she waiting for? I'd declared Gemma at her birth, although the ceremony to bind us had come much later, when she was old enough to agree. When the bond crackled in place, I'd known it was stronger than that of my first charge, who died during the war. The elders, what remained of them, confirmed the rare bond and said I should feel lucky. I certainly hadn't felt lucky when Gemma began sneaking out and finding her feminine power. While blocking her out completely was impossible, I dammed up the bond during her intimate moments.

Leana turned to face me, an unreadable look locked in place. She had to know. How could she not? I'd left with Gemma and not returned. I hadn't even tried to make contact, telling myself it was for Gemma's safety, which was true. That wasn't the only reason, though. I'd taken the cowardly approach, letting Casimir decide what information to feed across the forest. I told myself I'd done it to spare Leana the pain, but my actions were those of someone lacking courage. I'd left her frozen in limbo—at least I thought I had. Maybe she'd moved on, and if she had, I'd be thrilled for her. She deserved a love I couldn't give her.

"Cyrus?" My name crossed her lips in a cracked whisper, so broken my heart crumpled in response.

"It is me," I said out loud, not daring to enter her mind for fear she'd see the truth before I could explain it. She deserved to know, and I would tell her. She glamoured into her human form and picked Drew up in her arms. He was about the age for her to declare, although a bonding ceremony would have to wait until he'd lived enough fae years to return the declaration. Leana was clearly already connected to him. "Are the others here?"

"Yes," she said, glancing toward the wooded area at the base of the mountains. "Is Gemma safe?"

My heart twisted with guilt at Gemma's name, even standing here before Leana. Guilt that I'd left my bonded. Guilt that I'd loved another. Guilt that I'd created a mess and had to face the consequences. "She is safe and happy with her mate."

Leana's glamoured hand went to her chest, setting Drew on his feet. "Mate? Not husband?"

I'd assumed they would marry. He had proposed. I didn't know why they hadn't other than mate was a higher recognition, so maybe they felt it wasn't necessary. Plus, I'd heard from Casimir that their daughter, Daphina, named after Gemma's mother, was quite a handful. "No, he is her true mate."

"Maybe that is a good sign for us," she said, turning to walk toward the wooded area. She held Drew's hand and guided him. "Are you coming?"

I remained in my natural form and followed. "Drew, I have not seen you since you were a tiny thing."

He looked up at me but didn't say a word.

"He's a bit shy. He just started talking again right before..." She glanced down at Drew, and his eyes widened. "Everything happened."

"Of course," I said. "I've been with your big sister, Gemma." I cringed at my word choice. "Do you remember her?"

He studied me with his big hazel eyes and nodded enthusiastically. "What's your name?"

"I'm Cyrus," I said and nudged his head with my muzzle.

He smoothed his hair down as if I'd done his wind-blown locks a disservice.

I chuckled and turned to Leana. "How many are here?"

"Every one of us from the prison kingdom made it here. Albert has been too consumed with Arianna's power to even give our kind a thought. Some fae made it out with us."

The tightness in my shoulders eased, hearing we'd had no losses. When my brother reached out, he hadn't had time to give me all the details—just that the magic

General Daphina had woven into place had finally come down, and Albert was himself after two hundred years. My twin had conveyed that Gemma, her family, and Arianna were all safe, and Leana had gotten their brother, Drew, out. Marius had to go after Ari, and I was to retrieve Drew. The siblings had only I hadn't been sure what state I would find our people in when I got to the meeting place.

"He will come for our tears and our horns," I said, remembering the slaughter he'd instituted with the vampires during the Great War. Bitterness for the lives lost, both unicorn and fae, that I'd long buried surfaced. I tugged on my magic to fill the space with peace and drive out my anger. "It's the only way he will stand a chance against Arianna's power."

"So, it's true? She is blessed."

"Nyx has granted Arianna her full power. Arianna has not come into all of it yet. The Goddess saw fit to hide them within her granddaughter until they are needed."

"That has its dangers too. How will she train and prepare for the war her father will bring?"

Unicorns emerged from the woods, and I held my mental shield up against our collective consciousness. I'd hoped to speak with her before engaging the others. Marius already knew what happened between me, Gemma, and Laurel, but my brother could guard parts of his mind from the others while listening to our mental exchanges. I had not earned that gift, nor did I deserve it. Many saw my leaving with Gemma as a betrayal of Marius, as I didn't give him the courtesy his rank deserved. Even then, I knew things were different between

Gemma and me from the other bonded. I missed her presence in my mind, but if I let the wall down, it would only hurt her and Laurel. They had a family now. A beautiful daughter who would be a gifted ruler one day. And Leana would see exactly what my thoughts were. She needed to hear it from me, not with the rest of unicorn-kind.

CHAPTER 2

LAST TEAR

A group crowded around us in the camp. It was impressive what they had done in the short time since Rainier had retrieved Arianna. Marius had gotten them organized quickly when the fae prince's plans changed. Rainier earned the credit for how he'd held the vampires at the border for so long with only scouts slipping through, and Casimir had told me he blamed himself for the timing faux pas. It could have happened to any of us, though. War meant making fast decisions, and his quick thinking likely saved Arianna's life—and the lives of the unicorn and fae here in front of me. I couldn't keep my conscious wall up forever around the camp. It would raise suspicion, because I was not our leader. The time to have the conversation with Leana I dreaded was now.

"Shall we go somewhere to talk?" I asked her.

She nodded, her mouth set in a firm line. "Let's go down by the river. It's peaceful and no one will be there at this time."

"And Drew?"

She motioned for an older fae woman I recognized from the kitchen. "Can you give Drew some of those treats you made this morning? I'll be back in a little while."

"Of course, Leana," the gray-haired woman said.

The walk to the river, short and silent, took a few minutes. Leana didn't release her glamour, keeping her faelike form instead. Everything in my four legs told me that she already knew what I planned to share with her.

I paused at the riverbank, listening to the water gurgle. The river, calmer this time of year, left the sounds of the forest audible. Birds rustled in the trees, settling in for the night. A bear foraged off in the distance. The sunset drew my attention most. The deep oranges, pinks, and golds radiated in a magnificent kaleidoscope this evening. I glamoured into my human form, thinking of how Gemma looked in the soft glow of a sunset. Memories flooded in, and I let them take hold. The raw emotion overwhelmed me, but I wanted to be truthful with Leana. I couldn't do that hiding from it myself. I turned my face up into the warmth of the light. "It's been a while since I've seen one so beautiful."

"It is a glorious dusk." Leana's voice cracked. "Years, Cyrus. Years have passed."

I glanced over to see a tear crest the lower lid of her big brown eyes and hang in her lashes. I caught the magic liquid as it dropped. "Do not waste your gifts on me. I am not worthy."

She turned to me. Pain dulled her usually bright eyes. I wanted to ease her hurt, say I was sorry for what I'd done, but I wouldn't invalidate my time with Gemma and Laurel that way. Instead, I held out my hand for her to take the tear, but she didn't.

"Keep it."

"I cannot, Leana."

"So, it is true. The rumors. The flashes of the future I saw. You and Gemma..." Her voice broke.

I squeezed my eyes shut. She already knew, and it made me feel less than that she heard it from someone else. Marius wouldn't have, so that left Casimir. I turned completely to face Leana. She gave me a pleading look that told me how selfish I'd been. "I loved her. It is true. I loved her in a way I didn't think I could."

"And what of us?" She stared out at the disappearing sun, the vibrant colors turning to a translucent gray.

The only thing I could offer her was a release of our involuntary union, and maybe she would find another to pair with. My words would hurt her, but I'd already done that. She needed hope for a future without me. "I will not force you to remain with me. We were never a match, and you deserve to find a unicorn who is."

"It doesn't matter to you that I love you?" Leana's voice broke on the last word like someone who hadn't been forced into a paired match as we'd been.

My heart ached, and I closed my eyes. None of this was fair to her, and I wished I could see the future to know what to say. When I opened them, I readied myself to ask the honest questions that had gone unsaid for too long. "Does it matter to you that I can't love you back? Is that the relationship you want to be in for a thousand years?"

"No, it's not." She inclined her head toward my hand and took her tear back into her body with her horn. "I'd hoped you would come to love me, but it seems destiny determined your heart would belong to Gemma. When do you return to her?" She wasn't angry, but her sadness seeped into the air around us, tasting almost like I'd eaten something sour.

The latter might be because hers mixed with mine as I thought of how to answer the question. "I will not. Just as you love me and it's not to be, so it is with Gemma for me. She is mated, and I'm her bonded."

She tilted her head to the side. "You didn't break the bond? Neither of you?"

"No, I closed off the connection, so she wouldn't have me in her head while she built her family." Breaking the bond with Gemma would have put her in pain, and she'd been pregnant when I left. I wasn't sure how that kind of magic disruption would impact her pregnancy. At least that was what I told myself. I think the real reason was that I didn't want to live in a world where I wasn't tied to her in some way.

"You are truly an idiot, Cyrus." She crossed her arms. "Maybe you couldn't love me because you are meant for something more. There is always a reason for our path, and most of our pain occurs when we ignore that calling."

I blinked a few times. A lot of names had been hurled at me in my life, but I'd never been called an idiot. Her logic made little sense to me. What was I missing? "I'm not following."

"I asked Marius to put us together for the reproductive

pairings. I did that. I made the request even though I knew you only wanted to be friends. I was in love with you, and he hoped I'd be your chance at happiness."

The urge to console left a twang in my mouth because I knew I couldn't do it without patronizing her. She deserved authenticity. "I was happy, Leana."

"Just not in love," she whispered. "Until Gemma."

"Yes, but that doesn't mean I don't care for you and your happiness."

"I know," she said, her voice so quiet it proved hard to hear even with unicorn hearing. "So, what do we do now?"

"That's up to you. I'll support what you want." The conversation was going better than I'd expected, but the most important thing out of it was what Leana needed to move on.

"I want to declare Drew as my charge. He's too young for the bonding ceremony, but I want to make my intentions known. Marius had to abandon his attempt to retrieve him from here when Albert kidnapped Arianna. He said the volatile situation raised the risk. But where Drew goes, I will go as well."

"I'd expected as much based on what Marius had shared with me. Albert is still on the loose, and they were planning to make another attempt to capture the false king." I waited for her to look at me. Fear flashed across her features. "I saw the instant bond you had with Drew before I left. I'm surprised you haven't declared for him already."

"So, you will not stand in the way?"

"Why would I? It's the least I can do to support you, and I didn't ask your permission when I declared for Gemma."

"That's because her magic reached out to you from General Daphina's womb."

I nodded and let out a slow breath. Even in the womb, her magic had sought me out—sang to me as if the Fates were guiding me. The highest honor of my life was to be a protector for General Daphina's daughter. I didn't know then how things would evolve from the moment when we performed the bonding ceremony two decades later. Everything changed at that point—the way I looked at her, my feelings, how protective I was. Not once had I thought of her as anything other than my charge and a potential ruler of the fae kingdom until that day. The bond changed, and it had been like the wind had blown every-thing from the past away. Except, I was paired with Leana, and Gemma was my bonded charge. Nothing was to be done.

"Gemma named her babe after her mother?"

"She did." I relaxed, not realizing I'd held so much tension. An easy smile crossed my face. "I left before the child's birth, but Marius told me. He'd felt the power in the child from the moment of conception, just as I knew Gemma was pregnant."

Erebus, I regretted leaving even if I knew it was the right thing to do under the circumstances. They were a happy family. Casimir had told Marius bits of news to share with me. Gemma had taken a post to help the fae from the prison kingdom acclimate to the real fae kingdom—or reacclimate in many cases. They'd moved on without me, and I accepted that.

Leana jerked her head toward me. "It's not…" Her voice trailed off, but I knew what she wanted to ask.

"You and I and all of unicorn-kind know that is impossible. The child is half her mate and half her." My heart folded in saying it out loud. Even though I bore no responsibility from our bond, I wanted to be there to help Gemma and Laurel raise their daughter.

Leana stepped closer to the river. "There were stories once that the Goddess Nyx could grant such things."

"She might, but Nyx has long since left this world behind. And I would know if any part of the child were mine. I believe my role was to save them from the fate that General Daphina had nearly succumbed to." My bond with Gemma was like a living entity on its own. So much so, I'd almost missed the pregnancy. When I'd seen the tiny snippet of the future without me in it but with a way to save her baby, I knew it had been Nyx and Erebus's wish that the baby live, and my destiny was complete. My heart broke like King Veran's crystal when he lost General Daphina for the final time.

"The birth? You gave her a tear."

If my tear saved Gemma and Laurel's daughter, then maybe that was my purpose in their lives. "I did, but I do not know if what I saw came to fruition. Marius only told me that the child lived, and that was enough for me."

Her face softened to a knowing expression. "And you don't wonder about her?"

A knot formed in my throat, but no tears fell. "Of course, I do, Leana."

"What about if we had been fortunate enough to have our own child? Would things have been different?" Her question held no desperation. Her demeanor remained calm as if she were inquiring about what was for dinner. I appreciated her compassion, given she was the only victim in this situation. She chose not to be, though. That was who she was.

I took her hand in mine and laid my other on top. "A child doesn't create love between the parents. The love is for the child, and while the parents might share that love, it doesn't mean it will give life in a relationship where there are no embers."

Leana watched me for a moment and gently extracted her hand. She cleared her throat. "We should return to the others. They will want to catch up with you too."

If she wanted to tell the others everything, I'd fall on that sword. I was the one who broke my vow as a guardian by falling for my charge and acting on it. The fault was solely on me. "You didn't say what you wanted besides Drew being your charge. Do we announce our separation so that you can find another?"

"No, let's just leave it as is and focus on our charges. That is what brings me the most happiness." She stared at me, and I saw the pain etched in her extraordinarily beautiful face. "And I suspect for you as well."

"Yes, but I cannot be there." My pain called to hers, and I hadn't shut it down quickly enough. I cursed myself for saying something so selfish in front of her.

She gave me a sad smile and let her glamour go. "You choose not to be in her presence and that of her family because it causes you pain. There is a difference." She paused. "You know the saying about our tears never hitting the ground."

"Yes, of course."

She took a couple of steps forward and stopped. "Does that mean we never cry alone?"

I chewed on that idea as I released my glamour. The only time I'd wept was during the war and when my parents died...until Gemma. "What do you mean, Leana?"

"Do you remember the rest of the saying?"

"Our tears are never meant to be bound. In the air, earth, fire, and water, they can be found, but never should they touch the ground."

"That is the version we teach the children, yes," she said.

I fell into step beside her on the trail. "There's another version."

She nodded. "That is the modern version our generation speaks. There is a more literal translation from an old text." Leana stepped over a bunch of flowers, careful not to trample them. "For we are the air, earth, fire, and water, thy powers shall never be bound until the last tear falls and our bodies lie in the ground. For when a tear has fallen for fate, our kind will once again proliferate."

"That's morbid and wrong. We've all shed tears for fate."

She stopped. Her solemn expression masked the trepidation rolling off her. "No, we have not. We shed tears for consequences and sorrow. You are the only one I know whose tear saved a child of Nyx's bloodline."

Leana inclined her head, walking toward the camp. I stood in place, pondering her words for so long my legs began to ache. *Had that been what my father meant?*

CHAPTER 3

OLD FRIENDS

I mingled among the others of my kind until the crowd was like a wall closing in around me. I needed space. After being away from contact for so long, it was smothering—so many scents, from roses to a few who needed to visit the stream. Either that or they required a lesson in hygiene. Then there were the stares and whispers. It was more than I could handle for the night. Marius was unreachable, but that was normal for him. I couldn't sleep, and being still invited thoughts of Gemma and Laurel, so I walked around the edge of the camp. Not that it stopped the thoughts, but the movement gave me something else to focus on. The moon filled the sky in a glorious cascade of light cresting through the trees around the site. The nocturnal animals stirred, and yellow eyes flashed in random blinks in the woods—nothing dangerous. They were curious.

"Cyrus?" I turned to see my old friend Cleave in his faelike form. His dark hair was longer, but with a similar curly style that the women loved for him to wear. A scar marred his warm brown skin on the forearm. None of us were immune to the reminders of the war we'd survived while others perished. Cleave hadn't been able to hold the glamour long when I'd last seen him, so I shifted into my alternate state as well.

I patted his shoulder. "Well gods be damned. I didn't think I would see you again, my friend."

"Nor I you. I thought you were dead, and Marius would never let us in on what he knew." He embraced me, and I appreciated the gesture. My brother let them believe I was dead, and I agreed with his decision as a way to protect the others and our charges. Even so, it stung.

"Ah, yes. The curse of being our leader. He gets to hear everyone else's thoughts, but we only hear the ones he chooses to share."

His gaze held concern. "It makes sense as a rule, but we were all left to wonder about you."

"I'm sorry for that and sorry my brother was put in that position. How are things here?"

"We need our leader and guidance, but he's off with Arianna."

The entire unicorn collective knew the importance of General Daphina's daughter, but I recognized the hint of frustration in his voice. I'd faced it myself on occasion. He was bonded to the future of our realm. That duty came first, even if we didn't admit that to the fae. "That is where he should be. She is just coming into the power Nyx gifted her."

Cleave loosed a breath. "That is understandable, but

we need a leader here. We are just existing and have been since the prison world came down."

They'd done far more. The camp was viable and efficient. A system to bring water to the camp had been established. They had shelter, and a cooking area. The setup was more than adequate. "I'll try to contact Marius to see what he advises."

My brother wouldn't ignore the immediate needs of our people for any reason other than the survival of all.

"Or," Cleave said, holding his hands up in a defensive posture, "hear me out. You step in."

I scoffed. "No one will want me. I've been gone for over half a decade."

"It might surprise you, then, that there are those who want to follow you."

"You think?" I pondered his suggestion. While I'd led our kind and fae during the war, I wasn't built for leadership like this. Marius inherited the role, but he was more than born for it. He could govern, organize, and make decisions faster than it took most others to understand a situation. No option existed without speaking to my brother first. I needed to know what he saw for the future of unicorns and the fae in our care at the camp.

"When you arrived, many wondered if you returned to lead us in his absence."

They had to have believed I'd come back to Leana if I was alive. Or maybe they understood more than I realized. "I will consider serving our people as my brother's proxy, but only if he approves of this decision. Did he not leave anyone in charge?"

Cleave's face relaxed, and I saw hope in his eyes. "No. Everything happened so fast. I don't believe he had time to appoint anyone before the prince rescued Arianna."

I nodded. "He came back early from the front after the vampire infiltrated a camp on the far edge of the forest."

"Yes, and that set everything on a different path. The spell broke sooner than expected."

With my brother out of touch, our people were ill-prepared for the current events and had no clear guidance. "I'll take the role on for now and attempt to contact Marius and confirm he agrees with this decision."

One side of Cleave's mouth turned up as if he knew I'd acquiesce. "It will be best for all of us to have someone here who can give the collective direction. You look tired. Did you find somewhere to bed down?"

"Not yet. The day has been long, but I will stick close to Leana and Drew." I'd given my word to secure Drew's safety, and I intended to keep it.

"You're..." He paused. "Forgive me. I should not ask."

"We're still together if that is what you are wondering." The lie left a sourness on my tongue.

Cleave averted his eyes.

"There is no offense, my friend. I have been gone for some time."

"She has always been faithful to you, even when we were told to try to pair others."

My heart constricted so tight I thought it might burst. She'd been true when it wasn't required, and I'd loved someone else—not just a tryst but real love. I was a bastard of the worst kind. "I know she was. Leana has always been purer than most. She never needed guide rails to tell her the path she should be on. She chose her own."

"Since childhood, she stood out as a beacon of strength and perseverance." Cleave's tone was proud, and I remembered they'd been close as children.

"I forgot that you two had grown up in the same region."

"Yes, many, me included, always regarded her as the smartest and most beautiful of us."

"That she is," I said. "Speaking of, I need to go find her."

Cleave's expression looked as if he were in pain, and that made me think he knew more...maybe they all did. If that was true...if they all knew, then why would they want me as a leader? "I'll see you in the morning."

"Tomorrow." I turned in the direction I'd seen Leana wander off with Drew, following their scents.

"Like this, Leana?" A tiny voice carried on the wind and settled around me. It must be Drew's.

"Yes, you are doing so well." She knelt in front of him in her human form. Leana beamed with happiness.

I stood at the trees' edge as Drew performed low-level illusion magic. It was easy to start the elves at that point before their elements manifested. The power lived in their blood like a life force, but it remained hidden until ready to emerge into the world like a butterfly from a cocoon. I didn't sense immense power from Drew, but his father, Albert, had been similar. My kind missed the signs, rendering it too late when we saw the corruption in

Albert, and Leana would make sure that didn't happen with Drew.

"You can come forward, Cyrus," Leana called out over her shoulder. "Neither of us will bite."

I glamoured to my two-legged form and joined them in the small clearing. "Your illusion magic is quite good for your age, Drew."

He looked me up and down as if he sized me up for a fight, but he was too young for that. "I'm not a little kid anymore. I'm a big boy, and I do big-boy magic."

I pressed my lips together until I could speak without laughing. "Yes, you do. I can't wait to see what else Leana has taught you."

He looked at Leana as if asking for permission.

She nodded.

Drew took three big steps and jumped up high. With his little hand, he grasped the first branch, which had to have been six or seven feet off the ground. He swung back and forth a few times before floating back down to stand in front of Leana.

Shock rippled over me. It wasn't fae power—not at his age. "What kind of magic does he have?"

"It would seem his mother's heritage included a sprite or something similar."

"But they have been extinct for five centuries." Not much was known of Sion, but Drew's mother's beauty had often been described as ethereal, and he shared that same other-realm look.

"Or not."

"Does anyone else know?"

"No, only you and me. Drew knows that we only work on magic out of the prying eyes of others. Right, Drew?"

"It's just for us." He raised his head. "And now you, Cyrus."

I knelt to be level with him and tapped his nose. His enthusiasm was contagious, but I suspected my brother had known magic waited to awaken in this young boy. "Thank you for sharing how special you are with me. I promise I will abide by Leana's rule on it."

Drew laughed. "It's not a rule. It's an ag...agra... aggravation."

Leana giggled. "An agreement."

Drew's interest shifted to a leaf blowing along the ground. He chased it around in a circle with a hand out, trying to catch it. Thank Erebus, the child seemed to be coming out of the grief that had trapped him for years.

"As it should be," I said, hearing the awe in my voice. A sprite. But how? "Do you think his power could be a trace in the bloodline from before they died off?"

"I suppose it is possible. You saw him, though. That looked like more than a trace."

"It did." Still, it gave me hope for our situation. Sprites were one of the few types of fae who could intermingle with others—other fae, humans, unicorns, and they could even have children with vampires, who couldn't otherwise conceive. They were fertile people, so when the sickness took the sprites, it shocked the realm to see them die off so quickly. If Drew's manifestation of power was a remnant of the sprite gene pool, we might have a chance at survival if we understood how they were able to mix with others.

CHAPTER 4
SUBTERFUGE

Brother, can you hear me? I'm with the others. I reached down our twin bond. While twins were rare among our kind, the bond we had from our shared childhood experience was normal. The connection made some unicorns uncomfortable. It was similar to the shared communication of our people, but not close enough for them to approve, despite how favored my brother was.

Cyrus? His voice, faint but audible, meant he was a good distance away—too far for the others to reach him.

Who else can get in your head uninvited?

Arianna, but she's with me, and you sound different from her. I could hear the smirk in his thoughts, but there was a hint of trepidation too. I guessed he was worried about things here, or maybe his headstrong charge had him stressed.

I chuckled and let it flow down the bond to let him feel things were as good as they could be here. *Are you safe?*

For now. Arianna is so much like her mother.

The General would be proud to hear that.

She would. I can't talk long. Is everything okay there?

It's lacking in the leadership area, which is why I wanted to talk to you. How do you feel about me serving as your proxy here? I kept my thoughts natural, not wanting to overstep my place. I hated asking permission for anything, and we both knew it.

You are my brother. My twin. There is no one else I'd trust more than you to stand in as leader while I'm so far away. His thoughts flowed through with thoughtful kindness. Still, I sensed a distraction on the edge of his tone.

And you would tell me if you needed me? Needed us?

Yes. No assistance required right now, but I will put out the call should it be. Gemma is—

His thoughts evaporated as did our connection. *Marius? Gemma what? Marius?*

He was clearly far enough away that our connection could be too weak, but the sudden drop seemed more of a block, much like what I'd done with my bond to Gemma. A sense of foreboding settled over me. If Gemma was hurt, he would have told me right away. I reasoned that it was probably Arianna's magic going awry as it so often did.

"Are you okay?" Leana's voice drifted around me.

"Yes," I said, the word coming out harsher than I intended. "Apologies. I didn't mean it that way. I am fine."

She waited for me at the edge of the path. "You were speaking with Marius I see. You're always agitated after speaking with him."

"My brother has granted me his proxyship here for now." He still trusted me, despite my broken oath. It would all eventually come out, and my dishonor would belong to no one but me.

Leana let out a long breath. "We need some leadership for our people, so that is a good thing. Many are scattered, and others are lingering close to the vampire border to monitor activity."

"There is much to do then. Will you help me?"

"I will, but you need a second who doesn't have a charge, especially one as young as Drew."

"Where is he?" I asked, scanning around to see if he was hiding somewhere.

"He's with the cook." She tilted her head and smiled. "I'm sure he has begged a dozen sweets from her by now."

I chuckled. Gemma's sister, Arianna, had a thing for chocolate when she was younger too. "From what I remember, the sweet tooth runs in their family."

"It does." She sniffed a bunch of wildflowers growing on the side of the trail in bright colors of yellow, blue, and red.

I'd expected her to jump at the opportunity for the position, but I was worried my transgressions might impact her decision. She knew her mind. Always had. She'd been viewed as a leader before I left...but her bond with Drew had grown stronger. Leana had changed and so had her priorities. "Any suggestions for who should take the second-in-command position?"

"Cleave has always been loyal and trustworthy. What

about him?" Leana's earnest tone matched the reaction in my gut.

"I did connect with him last night. He was the one who suggested I take the lead here for Marius."

"He's already thinking like a second. He'll be a good choice."

"Yes, I suppose he will. Walk with me to find him?"

"Of course."

The soft vegetation of the forest mushed against my hooves and made a slight sucking noise. The atmosphere of these woods weighed quite differently from the Forgotten Forest, where everything felt dead...not to mention spirits weren't trapped here. The Forgotten Forest was a place of great tragedy, and many fae and unicorn perished on the land. If we had the power of General Daphina, unicorns could have helped her release the souls to Nyx's realm, but that wasn't meant to be. Maybe her namesake would be able to one day when she came into her power.

"You've always been quiet, Cyrus, but you seem more so now."

"My head is filled with things to do and worries for our people." And thoughts of my happiest days, but I didn't voice that.

"And for Gemma?" A flicker of pain penetrated her forced smile.

Why is she asking about Gemma? It only hurts us both. Does she know what my brother tried to tell me? "You don't need to keep bringing her up, Leana. What happened is done. I will not speak of it to anyone here."

"I was thinking last night that there is always a reason for the way things happen, so there was a reason, and maybe yours was to save the child. She has General Daphina's name and certainly will have her power. She could be the one to restore all our glory."

My lungs tightened like when I'd been on the battlefield. General Daphina's granddaughter would not face the same fate she had, not as long as my four hooves touched the soil of this realm. I pushed the war memories back and grounded myself in the present, focusing on the vibrant colors of Leana's mane. Gemma and Laurel's daughter wasn't the only gifted fae child. "Your new charge certainly has some interesting powers."

I was eager to learn more about Drew's sprite heritage. With their disappearance, many of the gifts they'd had became lore. If he had some of those talents, there were a host of ways he could help when he was older.

"He does," she said, her tone cautious.

"I'd like to find out more about his mother and her line."

"Albert brought her back from an excursion to the northern border toward the human lands." Her anxious tone matched the worry lines that creased her fine face.

I'd heard a different story and never questioned it. The alternate version I'd been told said she came from a small village in the kingdom. "She didn't come from part of the prison kingdom's population?"

"No, he kept much of that a secret. Only a few knew. He said the subterfuge was to protect her from court, but we know even with General Daphina's magic, pieces of the real him still came through."

I didn't bother to hide my shock. Access to the king was limited, but my uncle and Marius's closest friend were assigned to Albert. They should have shared the info, but perhaps Marius had blocked it from the collective. But why? "Do you think he knew then? About her?"

"Possibly. He did seem to truly love Sion. He mourned her until the day the magic broke, though not as he did General Daphina."

"Have you any knowledge of what sent him north in the first place?"

"No, the courtiers planned the entire trip under the heading of Court business. There were no formal announcements or processions when he left."

"Interesting. Is it possible he'd already broken free of the magic before Arianna's rescue?"

"I don't think so, but there were moments when the magic weakened that I could see the change in his eyes. As far as I know, no one else noticed the nuance—he'd squint slightly until his expression became a bit cruel. However, his dark look would just be gone as the power ramped back up. I'm assuming that occurred when it would draw from Arianna."

"So, his marriage to Sion could have been a mission. This could be a mission. We could be unknowingly..." I let my thoughts trail off because it was absurd to think that child was anything other than a little fae boy. But if Albert had been awakened from General Daphina's magic, even if

Leana hadn't known, it meant we could be playing right into his game.

"Drew is good, Cyrus. He's a kind, sweet boy whose life has been ripped apart multiple times by loss—first his mother, then Gemma, then Arianna."

"But you are his constant." I smiled at her. "His stability."

"That is what I do best." She lifted her chin but looked away. "Be the rock when everyone else is gone."

Those words stung me to my core. I'd left her in a vulnerable position, and she'd done so much more than survive. She'd thrived. She was truly the best of us, even if she wouldn't say it or see it for herself. Drew was another example. She didn't have to take him on, but she gave him the love and nurturing he needed in the absence of his biological family. She was gifted in a way that I would never be, could never be, with my hardened heart and the love I could never have so far from my presence.

"Is there anyone else I could speak to who would know about Drew's mother?"

"There was a cook who was in the palace while Sion carried Drew, but I've already spoken to her. She didn't have any information we didn't already know. Perhaps you remember her from the kitchen? She made the best pies from the mountain berries when they were in season."

Something in my gut told me there would be more dead ends than helpful leads. "I remember a cook who made one just for you because she knew how much you loved them."

Leana smiled, and it was a true smile that the morning sun glinted off of. "She remembers everyone's favorites. She's the one who makes the little chocolates Drew loves." Her forehead bunched up. "Everyone is protective of Drew, Cyrus."

"As they should be. He's a vulnerable child."

She nodded, but something on her face gave me caution.

CHAPTER 5
NO BOWING

As I followed the sound of laughter and hammering, I noticed the stares as I passed through the camp. Cleave worked with a few others of our kind I didn't know well. They were glamoured into faelike forms to build some temporary shelters designed to offer a semblance of privacy. He introduced me to the others, but they made their hurried excuses to leave.

"Do I need a bath?" I sniffed the air.

"No, it's nothing like that."

"Then what?"

"They know of how heroic you were in the war and of your many triumphs. You are a legend as much as your brother."

I snorted. "I doubt that. My brother is the kind who is written about in history. I'm the kind who is forgotten."

"You don't believe that, do you?" Cleave asked, his tone skeptical.

Did I? My contributions weren't on the same level as my brother's. He embodied greatness with every stride and placement of the hoof. Even before he was named our leader, unicorns looked at him in such a way. I'd always just been his brother. "My brother is the best leader our kind has ever known. Being a distant second or third or fourth or more from him is still a great honor."

"Cyrus, you are too modest of your own doings. You have given to our people, to the fae people, and to the world a piece of your soul. That can never be diminished."

"Since you seem to think so much of my accomplishments, is now a good time to ask a favor?"

"Ask anything you wish. I'm more than happy to offer my services." His smile had something behind it that I couldn't place.

"I spoke briefly to Marius this morning, and he is in agreement that I shall serve as his proxy here."

"That is great news, but what does that have to do with me?"

"If you will, I'd like for you to serve as my second-in-command."

He shifted his weight. "Isn't Leana the obvious choice?"

"Perhaps, but she is taking on a young charge soon, and that will require her time. I'd be pleased if you would fill the position."

His smile broadened. "I'm very honored you have asked this of me. I will gladly take on the role of your second." Cleave dipped his head down in the way the unicorns bowed to my brother. Marius hated it but allowed the tradition so they could show their respect. I didn't deserve such reverence.

"Please, no bowing and no bowing from the others either. I am doing this for our people, not for accolades."

"I understand, but I think the people might feel differently."

"Let's set an example that we don't bow here for a proxy...only for the true leader—Marius."

"As you wish," he said. "What is first on our agenda?"

I surveyed the makeshift structures they had been working on when I found them. The construction was simple and fine for the summer, but the openness of the temporary cover wouldn't be enough when colder weather arrived. "We need to get some better shelters in place. Even with our magic, the coming winter will be hard on us, and we are not used to it. Then, we need to talk about contacting those we've been separated from in the fae kingdom."

"And across the other borders."

"I heard some of us were hidden in the human lands, but they had moved on when the vampires invaded. Is that the latest?"

"To the best of my knowledge, a few of us are still there, but most have returned or moved on to other areas where they felt safer. Establishing communities with our dwindling numbers has been difficult. The reproductive pairings have left a bad taste in some, and they vacated for that reason as well."

"Hmm..." I understood that all too well, and while I recognized the risk for our line, I would be a hypocrite by condemning their personal decisions. "I can see how that would be difficult for many. We are used to having our choices and taking any away would be hard, especially when it comes to love." I lowered my voice. "We are facing extinction. Are those who are against the pairings accepting complete disappearance as our fate?"

"I don't know the details, but I think they believe in some ancient text they found that said we would be saved." Cleave kept his voice low, matching mine.

I'd heard of the writings, and the more radical of our kind intended to weaponize them more than once in our history. "Those texts are subject to interpretation and weren't written by us. They were the scribblings of fae."

"Fae with foresight. Albeit limited."

"This is going to be challenging, isn't it?"

"If it were me, I'd focus our efforts on those here first and worry about the radical ones later."

His counsel was a similar strategy to what my father taught me and Marius. Cleave needed to know I trusted him and saw his value. "You are right. That is good advice, Cleave."

"Thank you. I'm glad that I can live up to my role on the first day."

A sweet, rich aroma floated in the air. "What smells so good?"

"The cook is making candies from some of the things we gathered. They want to celebrate your return."

I studied him to see if he was joking. Cleave seemed completely serious. "I've done nothing worthy of cele-brating,"

"You have returned to us. Is that not reason enough?"

Not only did I not deserve this recognition but it also made me uncomfortable. "But there are many others who have returned and still many more who have not."

"This is about you." He grinned. "And I might have alluded to you possibly taking on the position of leader while Marius is away."

A rumble came from deep in my chest. "You did what? That wasn't yours to tell. You had no way of knowing if I'd talked to my brother or not."

"But it all worked out. You did speak with him, and he did agree with the suggestions."

I nipped at the air near his carotid artery. He didn't flinch as if he sensed my bluff. "In the future, these communications will come from me unless otherwise noted."

"See. You are already in leader mode."

His confidence in me bolstered my own, but he needed to learn to treat conversations with more sensitivity in the future. The time we'd spent on a battlefield was long ago. He hadn't held a leadership position to my knowledge, so I'd let this go as a learning experience for him. Father had chastised me many times before I learned my lesson on what to keep to myself. Our situation didn't allow for a long learning curve. I'd have to spend more time with Cleave to train him in tactics to guard his thoughts and his words. "Let's get to work."

CHAPTER 6
UNWORTHY

I followed Leana's scent to find her with Drew on the far edge of the tree line where the mountaintop came into view. Power practically flowed from the sierras. The air charged with the arcane magic in a way that I didn't feel while inside the trees, almost as if the foliage provided some barrier from the immense force.

"He means well, Cyrus," Leana said in her faelike form before I even asked my question. She sat cross-legged on the bright green grass in front of Drew. He mirrored her position but hovered about two inches off the ground.

"When did he gain the power of levitation?"

"I think the fright around recent events triggered it. It first manifested when we arrived here." Her watchful eye never left the young boy.

I stared up at the mountains around us and glamoured into my alternate persona. I squatted down and grabbed a handful of the soil, letting it drift through my fingers and inhaling the sweet aroma of decay. These lands had been inhabited by sprites at some point, at least according to the legend we heard as younglings. That connection could have triggered the reaction in Drew as well. I followed the curve of the mountain to the indentation said to have been the sprite homelands. No one dared enter there, much like the Forgotten Forest. The elders thought the area to be a graveyard now.

Only, it wasn't ghosts they feared but more they avoided the chain of peaks out of respect. I'd never been there, but my father used to tell Marius and me stories of how beautiful the valley nestled between the three massive mountain peaks had been. He'd attended many seasonal festivals there in his lifetime. From what I'd heard, more than a little debauchery occurred during those parties, but he, like most of our kind, believed in freedom to love all who loved you—the only forbidden lines were mates and charges.

I was the odd hoof out in that I had never loved anyone except Gemma, and she was a charge for me and a mate to Laurel. Each time a memory transported me back to my time with my charge, the pain that lived in my chest since I left expanded a little more. I gritted my teeth until it passed. If I didn't keep moving, I would crumble. I'd never wanted to sleep with anyone the way I had Gemma. Some had caught my attention, but the attraction was different when I did fuck a few from time to time. There had been no one in my solitude since I made love with Gemma and Laurel. While I didn't have those feelings for Leana, she'd been more than a fuck. She deserved better than whatever the hell the few times we'd been together had been.

"Horn to Cyrus. Where'd you go just now?" Leana asked.

If I could do nothing else, I'd spare Leana from tales of my pining for another. It was bad enough that she caught me drifting off. "Remembering stories my father had told us of the festivals in the mountain."

She turned her head and looked toward where I'd been lost. "I don't know many of them. My mother's birth came after the sprites had left us."

I forgot how young Leana was for our kind. She'd barely been old enough to fight in the war. Her mother tried everything she could to get her to stay home, but she'd gone to follow me. My shame swallowed me whole. I suspected her mother knew what Leana could not see— that I'd never be able to love her the way she wanted.

Leana rested a hand on my knee. "We could go up there. It's probably not more than a day or two's journey. Or we could find a fae who can vanyshen."

I'd be lying to myself if I said I wasn't curious to see what was on the mountain. Answers to Drew's heritage might be there, but old sprite magic could be useful too. A quick trip to investigate what had Drew so curious couldn't hurt. He'd have two powerful unicorns to protect him.

"There are no fae here capable of such a feat. I've sensed none who have that type of power." Vanyshen allowed fae to jump distances, great and small. The gift came less and less to their kind, not all that different from how our births had dwindled. Vanyshen drew on old power, and our births were said to be reincarnation, so I imagined that took immense magic as well. It was all disappearing, though—us, their power, the veil between our realm and others'. Marius had to post a team to maintain the barrier between here and the human lands. Humans were far too weak and vulnerable for our realm. Their lives constituted but a blink of an eye compared to how long we lived. Occasionally, some fae would venture on the other side for certain medicinal herbs or other items. Some even fell in love and chose to stay. The human realm dampened all magic, and the fae would age more rapidly there—still a longer lifespan than the humans. It was like that realm was bleeding over into ours and sucking the magic from us. That wasn't the case, though, at least according to the elders.

"I suppose that is true. We could go. I can find someone to watch Drew for a few days." Leana rose and turned in the direction I faced. "But my intuition is telling me we should take him, and I don't know why."

"Let me think on it." There was much to do, but the mountain might have power we could use to save the realm. It could be the missing piece we'd been looking for since before the war.

Drew stood and followed our gazes. He pointed a tiny, little finger at the shadowed valley. "Home."

Leana and I exchanged confused glances. Her forehead bunched up, and her gaze darted between me and Drew, so I knew she hadn't instructed him to say the word. "Who told you to say that?"

Drew tilted his head to the side, looking at me like I should understand. Then he pointed to himself. "Me."

Goosebumps peppered my skin. Drew took on an otherworldly look. A light sting of power sifted through the air, and it wasn't fae.

Leana's brows scrunched together. "You told yourself?"

He shook his head as if to say no.

I knelt in front of him. "What do you mean, Drew?"

"Inside me. It's here." He pointed to his head.

"Are you saying you just knew it somehow?"

He nodded in agreement.

Fae received premonitions on occasion, although not as common as among unicorns, but I had no idea if sprites did. Father had often said they seemed to know the destiny of the realm, but that wasn't what Drew was saying. Or maybe it was the interpretation of a six-year-old.

"But how?" Leana looked at me like I should do something.

I shrugged. "I don't know."

"He's barely started speaking again, Cyrus, but the one thing he has never done is lie." Leana turned toward the mountain. "I'm going to see what's there. If for no other reason than for Drew."

She wasn't a weakling, but she would be vulnerable if she stayed in her human form for Drew. I couldn't let her go alone. I loosed a breath, already knowing what my decision would be. "Let's leave tomorrow. I need to come up with a truthful reason as to why the proxy is leaving the people when he just got here, and I need to introduce Cleave as my second-in-command."

"Tomorrow, then. That will give me some time to gather supplies."

I woke with a painful hard-on as I had nearly every day since leaving Gemma behind in an incredible act of self-ishness. The dream, when I slept deep enough for it, was the same. The fantasy, because that's what it had to be, played like a movie where Gemma, Laurel, and I joined. I allowed myself to fall into the memory of the deep connection that blossomed from our brief time moving as one unit. I crept away in silence from the camp.

When I made it far enough away no one could hear me, I glamoured into my alternate form, minus any clothes. Most of the time I suffered through until my dick gave up on relief. The dream had me revisiting my happiest and saddest moments—knowing what it meant to be in love. Those thoughts couldn't be at the top of my mind when I met with the other unicorns later. Nor could I walk in front of them with an engorged member. I gripped one of the trees and spit in the palm of my free hand. Stroking my cock in one long motion, I sank into the way Gemma's wetness coated my fingers. She'd been so ready to have both me and Laurel inside her. My gaze drifted down to my tight grip, and I pulled back, pushing the head of my cock through the hole my fae thumb and fingers made. I let my eyes drift close as I thought of how warm and tight the fit was when I'd nudged her entrance. Laurel's mouth had beckoned mine and electricity traveled down my spine as our lips met. Then, they'd both wanted my horn, and I knew I was ruined for anyone else after that. Our bodies melded together, and we all moved as one. 'Mine' slipped from my lips, but I was sure they hadn't heard me.

I swore under my breath as a knot tightened at the base of my spine just as it had that day. I stroked my hand faster for the release. A roar rumbled in my chest, and I clamped my lips closed. Warm liquid shot out from my cock and coated my hands. The relief would be temporary as it was each time, because I couldn't have the moment afterward to hold Gemma and Lauarel or tell them how much I cared for them. Nothing could repair the utter brokenness inside me that existed without them near.

After a quick wash in the stream, I walked toward the meadowy area where Cleave had assembled our kind by telling them I had an announcement. Marius handled crowds with grace, and I hated the focus on me. I wasn't ready to let them back into my head because I'd enjoyed the quiet. The proxyship provided a convenient reason to hold my ground and made keeping the status of my and Leana's relationship a secret. If I didn't know what dwellings we were accustomed to, I'd have thought the camp's setup was cozy. While I understood the fae's belief that the magic started depleting after the war, according to our elders, the truth was that it had started as soon as Nyx left this realm. The decline had seemed to increase exponentially, and the fae noticed, then they created their technology to subsidize the waning magic. The one thing the prison kingdom had done was maintain the older, simpler ways, but it was still a place of confinement and had to be brought down. I regretted that Albert had been allowed to live after the war. I'd been there, ready to end him with my horn, but he was fae and subject to their laws first. King Veran refused to end one of his favorites, and he paid the price for it like the rest of us. I shook my head to shake away the memories of the war.

Cheers erupted as soon as I stepped foot into the well-prepared camp. I waved and motioned for them to stop. Cleave came up to my side and leaned close.

"You don't have to make a speech, but I think they would appreciate it."

I hated speeches, and Gemma talked enough for the two of us in her youth. We were the perfect pairing. A hollowness formed in my chest as if I had a gaping war wound. I pressed my tongue to the roof of my mouth until my calm was restored.

"Thank you all for the warm greeting. It is a wonderful feeling to be back among my people. As many of you know, my brother is with his charge, who is very important to our future. He cannot be in both places, so I'm serving as his proxy—"

Shouts of support boomed out again, and I had to gesture for them to stop. The vocalizations were above and beyond what I'd earned, but their approval fortified my decision to step in on behalf of my brother.

"Cleave has accepted my request to serve as my

second-in-command during this time." The unicorns applauded for him. His warm reception, a good sign, reassured me of him as the choice. "I hope to reunite us with our scattered family as well as get us into a more sustainable position for Marius's return." All eyes focused on me, so many pairs I got lost in the sea of navy and black—for how long I'd disassociated, I couldn't say. Their hope emanated in their gazes and permeated my walls, and if it was possible, I felt even more unworthy. I swallowed hard. "Leana and I will be making a trek into some of the nearby areas over the next few days, and I hope to have some clarity for our future then."

Silence settled around us as the unicorns glanced at each other. The air charged with the slightly bitter taste of concern, matching their gazes. I might have lost their trust as easily as I gained it.

"We will endure and rebuild what we have lost."

Cheers erupted for a third time. Their trust intact, I was thankful to end this makeshift speech. If I never had to speak in this situation again, it would be too soon.

"What does Marius say of the nosferatu?" A female unicorn asked.

"Yes, what of the vampires? They've taken so many of us and many of the horses too."

I hadn't been ready to answer questions, but I should have anticipated them. *Stupid move.* The horses weren't related to us, but they, like many other creatures, were drawn to our magic. I didn't know what to tell them without striking fear or causing panic, and the numbers were so few that if the group was to scatter, they would be far less protected—fae and unicorn. The vampires could take any of them down if the odds were in their favor. "The vampires are invading our lands and the fae lands. Marius is our best hope at stopping them."

"Will we be expected to fight?"

"Not if we can avoid it," I answered, failing to evade the images of the Great War, as the fae called it. Loss trickled in, and I filled the cracks in the dam before it flooded me. No, we would not ask our people to face the nosferatu again if there was any way to prevent it. The call wasn't mine to make, but I knew Marius's heart on this topic.

"Are they close to us here?"

"No, they are in the human lands and on the other side of our lands for now."

"Good. Let them feast on the humans and not us," a large male unicorn I didn't know said as he stomped the ground. Anger swallowed any of the sorrow I hadn't hidden, but I dismissed his potential challenge.

"That is not our way, and we are better than that sentiment. Our blood gives the vampire something the humans can't. They will always want us more. The only way to guarantee our safety is to stop them."

"If it's the humans or us, let them have humans," the same male unicorn said.

I glanced at Cleave, and he was already sizing the male up. Although the warrior in me wanted to throat punch the insolent unicorn, we couldn't advocate for peace if we were violent among ourselves. I gave Cleave a slight shake of my head. The belligerent unicorn had the lean build of youth. I couldn't imagine being as callous as to make those statements, but this unicorn had grown up in a different time—a different world than I had. "I know many of you here were born after the Great War ended, and our existence was forever changed in those times. The unicorn philosophy still stands. It's what our kind has lived by for millennia. We are the protectors and only draw blood to save the innocent."

"And you believe that will save us?" a female unicorn asked. She looked familiar, but I couldn't recall her name.

"I do. My beliefs haven't changed over the last two centuries and are the same as they were before that. I will live by the legacy my father created and his father before him and his father's father before him." Invoking the legacy of leaders in my blood was an act I'd avoided in all parts of my life save the battlefield. I didn't do it lightly. The weight of their sacrifices for our survival sat heavy on my shoulders, but we were at a crossroads. The legends of my forefathers commanded respect, and I braced myself for what would come next—an act of obedience I didn't earn.

The group dropped and bowed their heads as if just invoking my ancestors' memories brought them to their knees. I glanced at Cleave to give him a dirty look, sure he'd instigated the bowing, but he lowered in reverence too.

"Please rise. I am no king nor your chosen leader. I'm just the proxy of Marius."

They remained in the low bow so long I thought they didn't hear me. Then, one by one, they began to rise until all stood in front of me. The respect cocooned me, and Erebus be damned, it felt good even though I'd done nothing to deserve it.

"I'd like to know what our status is. How many of us there are. How much in reserve we have for food for us and the fae. How far away we are from other splintered groups. Cleave, can you gather that information before Leana and I leave in the morning?"

Cleave smiled, an expression of pride and eagerness on his face. "Yes, that shouldn't be a problem. I'll have a report for you this evening."

"Thank you." I looked out over the crowd and saw a devoted following. My chest expanded with gratitude. "We will get through this and survive as we have. This isn't the first challenge our people have faced and will not be the last, but we will overcome these obstacles."

I wandered to the clearing Leana had used to practice with Drew. The space was vacant save for an older unicorn. One of our elders, judging by the solid gray mane and tail against his white and gray coat. I didn't recognize him.

"Hello." I lowered my head in respect.

"You shouldn't bow or shrink yourself to anyone."

I raised my head and met his sharp gaze. It looked as if a galaxy lived in his dark eyes. He wasn't just old. He was an elder. "I apologize that I do not know you."

"You can't know everyone, Cyrus." He curled his lips back in a grin. "I'm from distant lands."

"Are you an elder?" My gaze narrowed in on his, taking in the hints of silver in his black eyes.

He looked fucking ancient, but that seemed rude to say to an elder of our kind. "Do I look like one?"

"Yes, you do."

"Hmm. Then I must be." He laughed. "I'm glad you came here, to your people, but to this clearing as well."

"Why?"

"You have your own path to walk, Cyrus. Marius isn't the only one destined for greatness in your bloodline."

The constant unworthiness echoed in my mind in a hole of sadness, and I couldn't tamp it down fast enough. My bloodline would most likely end with me, but Marius would continue our ancestry with his children. "I'm not sure what you mean, but my brother is exactly the leader our people need."

"He is important, but so are you."

I studied him, finding him virtually unreadable except for his smugness. What did he gain by agitating me with this kind of talk? Maybe he had the disease some of our elders were afflicted with before their death. I wouldn't wish the terrible demise on anyone, including my worst enemy. Those sick with the illness of the mind could become violent, but he appeared calm and lucid. *If I just agree with his ramblings, he'll probably move on.*

"I waited for you here."

My warrior instincts kicked in, scrutinizing him. I

didn't detect a threat, though. "Did you need some assistance?"

"It is my assistance I offer you. Be wary of those who seek to be close to you. Not all are pure of intentions."

The only person I was close to here was Leana. She'd never betray me, despite how I'd hurt her. She approached all things unicorn with the goal of achieving the best outcome. There wasn't anyone else. "Leana is as pure as any unicorn can be."

"Hmmm." He twisted his mouth to the side and walked away.

I watched him until he disappeared into the thick woods. *What the actual fuck was he talking about?* Leana would never betray me or any unicorn, for that matter. She'd always believed in the greater good. How could he even suggest that she wouldn't be—especially right before we were to leave? Had he heard of our plans and wanted to stop us? If he was an elder and held knowledge that the rest of us didn't, he could keep it to himself until after the trip.

CHAPTER 7
VERANIQUE

Cleave found me down by the river. The midmorning light and the peacefulness of the calming song from the rippling water brought me to the spot. I tried to memorize every detail. Times would not remain harmonious for us for much longer. Between the meeting with the others and the strange encounter with the elder, my mind demanded a moment alone to recharge.

My second-in-command stood beside me. "There are three other clusters of our kind nearby—within a three-day trek. The rest have moved farther down to the southern border near the sea."

The coast was one of the most beautiful areas of the realm, with pristine white sand, which somehow never got too hot under the sun, and the water of beautiful, glittery blue, lighter than the aqua of the seas in the human lands. I had fond memories of my brother and me learning to swim in those waters. Families gravitated to the area, so

I could see why many would choose the location. Still, I had expected more to stay, but it didn't change our plans. "No one can blame them for that. If the choice is death or survival, some of us must live on for our species."

"No doubt. Those lands are the best in the world and far enough away to stand a chance." Cleave kept his voice low even though no one stood nearby.

I nodded. "And the other items I asked for."

"There are so few of us that we have plenty of food to get this group through a winter, but I suggest we find better shelter."

"Agreed. I think we should look at moving to the area where our denizens in Rainier's kingdom dwell." I'd considered our options. While most in that part of the realm resided outside the city limits, it was a central gathering spot. It gave us protection while still fulfilling our promise to help protect the fae. The downside of the decision was that if the vampires infiltrated, it would make us a buffet for them. I suspected the others would welcome the idea of reuniting with family and friends they hadn't seen in decades or centuries, in some cases.

"That's a good idea."

"Can you make the preparations while Leana and I are gone? I'd like to start moving that way. Judging by how short the days are, it will not be long before the weather changes and we are knee-deep in snow." While the cold wasn't uncomfortable for fae or unicorn, it dampened our magic. The elders' stories said it was the way used magic was returned to the elements. I didn't know if that was true, but when the snow melted, my magic came easier.

Drawing on the power with snow falling or blanketing the ground was like slogging through the quicksand in the Forgotten Forest. The fae city was warmer and rarely got snow, so that reduced our risks should an attack occur.

"I'll do my best to have them already to move. Some of these fae have never seen the technology in the city of Veranique."

I winced at the name. The city had no name since the king's death. "The crowned ruler renames the city with each reign. Veranique hasn't been used since King Veran died. The fae will be sensitive about that usage. Refer to it as the palace or seat of the fae kingdom for them."

"I'd forgotten. My apologies." Cleave lowered his head.

"No need to be remorseful with me." I glamoured to my faelike form and patted his shoulder. "As far as the fae who are unfamiliar with the advancements in the fae kingdom, I know it will be challenging. Unfortunately, we don't have the luxury of time to make easy introductions. Rainier does have some assistance set up for them, so we'll do the best we can when we get there. Can you send word ahead to expect us?"

"Of course."

"And Cleave?" I closed my eyes because the next words pained me. "Should we not return—"

"You will."

I held up a hand. "Should we not go on without us. We don't know for sure what we will find on that mountain, and if it is like the Forgotten Forest, there will be danger." After the battles I'd survived, few things struck me with fear. The unknown of the place unsettled me, but Drew's reaction and my gut feeling told me the answers we needed would be found there.

"It's not the same."

"Our kind hasn't stepped foot on that land in a millennium. We don't know what waits for us."

He glamoured to his alternative form like me. Standing tall, he placed a hand on my shoulder and looked me in the eyes. "You will make it back because our people need you."

I grasped his shoulder in the same gesture. "Until then."

LEANA PREPPED several packs of supplies while I met with Cleave and gave the final directions to the camp. She'd positioned a pile on the outer edge of the tree line where she and Drew waited for me.

"And you're sure you have enough food for the boy?" I looked over the packs and chuckled.

If eyes could shoot daggers, hers would have dealt a brutal death to me. "I've been taking care of him for years. I think I know his needs."

I pressed my lips together to keep from saying something else wrong. She'd been agitated all morning, and I knew there was more to it. She was nervous about the trip up the mountain, even though she wanted the trip as much as Drew did. The signs prompted us to take Drew with us and couldn't be ignored. Our journey was meant to be for three.

"I can't guarantee this will be an easy trip, but I will lay down my life to protect us."

"I know you will," she said, a grim smile on her face. "Let's hope it doesn't come to that."

"Ready?"

She nodded and shifted into her normal form. I lifted Drew onto her back, and he giggled as he sank his hands into her mane for a grip.

"Hold on tight." I patted the boy's hand.

"I'll hold him in place."

I grinned at her. "He doesn't know that."

She huffed. "He knows to trust me, and he can hear us."

Of course, he could hear us. I hadn't spoken through the mental connection. The trip must have her more distressed than I'd realized.

"Let's go." Drew thrust one hand in the air and pointed to the shaded valley of the mountain.

"Hold on with both hands." I winked at him and let my glamour go.

Being on four legs was so much better. I set a steady pace. We should arrive in the valley tomorrow evening. Leana and I could go straight through, but we'd decided to take breaks and camp for the night for Drew's sake. He would tire much more easily than we would. My apprehension resided with the mountain itself, and it made more sense to have a comfortable Drew than an agitated one with no sleep.

"Cyrus?" Leana's cautionary tone carried a hint of anxiousness. "Do you think everyone is here for the same reason?"

"You mean the unicorns in the encampment?"

"Yes, some are so distant."

The unnamed elder's message about the untrustworthy among us came to mind. *Had a fracture formed among the small number of us here?* I was sure Cleave would have mentioned it if the others gossiped about a split in ideology. "There is no way to know unless they tell us or we see it in the collective, but I think we all want our species to survive."

"You still haven't dipped into the collective."

It was a statement, not a question, because she would have known. "No, I'm not ready."

"You want to spare me the humiliation, but you don't have to. I release you from the request I made to keep our end between us. I chose to go to Marius for this pairing. Our failure is on me," she lamented, her tone honest.

Erebus, save me. My stomach sank. I'd talk about it as many times as she needed, but I wouldn't let her bear the guilt of the situation for one second. "There is no failure, Leana. In theory, we should have been a perfect match."

"But the Fates had other plans."

"So it would seem. I'm thankful for you, Leana, and the unicorn you are. I do care about you."

"I know you do. I just wish it could be more."

Before my feelings changed for Gemma, I'd asked Erebus to make me fall for Leana. After I fell for my charge, I knew that prayer was never going to be answered. A pang shot through my chest and down my back. I missed Gemma and Laurel, and I was sure this was what it felt like for a heart to physically break. Imagining life without them brought a similar agony. "That has been on my mind, too, but there is no changing what has happened. I must live with that."

"There is one thing." She glanced at me. "You could go to Gemma after we get our people to a safe place."

My heart twisted like a thousand knives had shredded it. "I made a promise to their family to leave."

"Did you consider that you might be a part of their family and, even bigger, a part of their destiny?"

Sorrow seeped into my chest and soaked into the shredded pieces of my heart. "Where is this coming from?"

"Last night, I remembered an old prophecy where a unicorn and a fae would create a new world. What if that is you and Gemma?"

I shuddered. Shock rocked through me that she even came to that conclusion. Marius was the twin destined to save the world, not me. "If anyone, that would be Marius and Arianna."

"It couldn't be them. Those in the prediction shared a bond like yours and Gemma's, not the mentorship like Marius has with Arianna."

Marius's relationship with Arianna had always been different. He was protective like a parent more than a guard, as if he had to fill in the gaps Albert couldn't. I never treated Gemma like a delicate moonflower. Her training prepared her for a future we hadn't predicted, but the love was more—more than any love I experienced with anyone. Marius had never mentioned this prophecy, so he might not have known it existed. It might have some useful information. "I can't even consider it now. Maybe when we are settled, I'll look at this prophecy and see what it says."

"You should do more than that, but at least it's a start."

She wanted me to be happy, that had to be it, but she would be wrong. I could never have the two fae who would truly bring me happiness. I wished a life full of joy for Leana, though.

WE MADE CAMP, including a tent large enough for the three of us, for the night at the edge of a small grove. Large animals were known to roam this area, and I wanted some protection should any come upon us.

I glamoured into my faelike form and made a fire. The temperatures didn't dip low enough to bother me and Leana, but Drew needed the extra warmth.

"Is he asleep?"

Leana, also in her human form, joined me on a log. She left the flap to the tent open to let the heat flow in for Drew. She smiled and nodded. "He's out."

I stoked the fire and watched the embers glow red. "I'm going to make another pass through the area to make sure we don't have any unexpected neighbors or visitors."

"We'll be here." She seemed more relaxed with just the three of us than at the encampment. I wanted to ask her if she was overwhelmed by the collective's thoughts, too, but I recognized I didn't deserve to ask her any questions. Besides, I wasn't sure I wanted to hear the answer. If she said no, then it was another example of how I was different. If she said yes, then it was a reminder that they gossiped about her because of my wrongdoings.

I took my time picking through the area looking for sleeping bears or nocturnal hunters. None made their presence known that I sensed or saw. Expelling some of my pent-up energy would have been nice, but it was a relief that no threats lingered around our camp. I stepped into the clearing and looked up at our destination. The moon shone in a waning crescent, and the valley amongst the peaks was barely visible in the dim light. Nostalgia filled my soul. Our father, mine and Marius's, took us out at night to remind us of the goddesses and gods who no longer walked our realm—especially of Erebus. Those were the times life was easiest, and my father imparted his wisdom on us. I could use his insight. I turned my head up to the stars as we so often did to feel closer to our ancestors.

"Father, am I on the right path? I feel as though I've made a mess of my life and Leana's and Gemma's too. How do I know that I'm headed in the direction I am meant to be?"

I closed my eyes and inhaled the night air heavy with dew. The scent took me back to when Marius and I were younglings. Father would take us out on regular visits around the kingdom and across the borders to others. He wanted us to be so aware of the world around us that it became second nature to welcome in new people and new cultures. Maybe that's why I'd fallen so easily for Gemma once I let my guard down. I didn't have the barrier to other species that many of my kind did. Most understood how the symbiotic nature was required for us to exist with the fae, but once the bonding rituals were no longer mandated, the majority left for a more reclusive existence. How Marius maintained the strong connection across the realm once he bonded with Arianna remained a mystery. Most of us couldn't connect across those long distances after we had a bond in place. His appointments came swiftly for those who would serve as his representatives around the kingdom. I suppose he never expected to need one here in our rightful home.

A stick cracked behind me, but I sensed the tiny presence who approached. I turned to see Drew rubbing his eyes. Leana wasn't with him, and I wondered how he got past her. "I thought you were asleep."

He raised his arm and pointed a finger to the mountain —specifically to the valley between the peaks, but he didn't speak.

"We'll be there tomorrow evening. I'm hoping we make it by sunset."

"Me," he said, his tone insistent.

I glanced back at the mountain. A tiny glimmer of light caught my attention. I squinted in the direction, trying to focus on where I saw it, but the light disappeared. *Had I imagined it?*

"Me," Drew said again. I looked to him and then to the valley.

The flicker of light danced again, confirming I hadn't conjured it in my head. Something or someone resided on the mountain, and the elders claimed no one inhabited it.

This mission just got more dangerous.

CHAPTER 8

THE LIGHT

I opened up a small piece of my mental barrier, removing one brick of my wall and focusing on the one person I wanted to reach, a task that took near singular focus. *Leana. Come to the clearing. Drew is with me.*

On my way. A rustling noise came from the side, and she appeared in her glorious unicorn state.

She studied Drew first before turning her gaze on me. Her forehead scrunched up. I inclined my head toward Drew. *Wait. Watch.*

She gave me a nod and focused on Drew.

"Me," he said, almost on a perfect interval with the cadence of the other times. The light flashed again.

Leana gave a little gasp. *What does it mean?*

I don't know. To my knowledge, no one has witnessed this but us. Drew seemed to sense it. He came out here on his own, and that's all he's said.

Should we be worried? Desperation drenched her thoughts.

It doesn't seem to be moving from the valley, so I think we're safe here. I'm not so sure about what will happen when we reach the mountain.

And you can't tell what it is?

No, it's too far away for me. What about you?

She shook her head. *I can't.* "Drew, let's go back to sleep. We still have a long journey ahead of us tomorrow."

As if breaking from a trance, he turned to Leana with his arms outstretched. She glamoured into her human shape and picked him up. "You are getting so big."

He laughed as if he hadn't been standing here like an obsessed vampire focused on its prey. *Could it be vampires? No, they have no need of light.* Unless they wanted to draw us in, and that could be the case. The vampires did set traps for unicorns, but we were far away from any sightings of them, so that felt less likely. Whatever we'd seen, I wasn't sleeping tonight.

I WATCHED the light flicker by for most of the night, and a couple of hours before daybreak, it stopped. My senses shifted into high alert because as long as it moved, I had a line of sight and didn't worry for the safety of my people. When it stopped, my instincts took over. I patrolled a hundred-yard perimeter around where Leana and Drew slept. The distance was short enough I could cover it in seconds but far enough I could stop anything I came across before it could get to them.

Once dawn broke, I let the tension go and rolled my head around, loosening the muscles in my neck and shoulders. I returned to wake Leana and Drew.

Leana's cautious look disappeared as she gently shook Drew awake. "Are you hungry?" She shifted to her human form immediately to take care of him.

"Chocolate," Drew yelled as he took off in a sprint. He ran behind a tree to take care of his personal needs. He seemed to be back to himself, but I worried about him wandering off.

"He's fine," Leana said as if she could read my thoughts.

"A little pond sits up ahead. We can wash up some and eat near the bank if you want."

Leana studied me for a moment, and I could see the fear from last night return to her features. Her alarm was justified, especially given a child was with us. After watching the light all night, I didn't think it was a threat, but I couldn't be sure.

I studied the shadow of the peak where the light had been visible. "We don't know what the light is. We'll be extra cautious as we continue forward."

She glanced at Drew. "It's not me I'm worried about. I've never seen him like that."

After I'd had some time to watch the light and think about Drew's behavior, I was convinced it was some type of ancestral call. What it meant, I didn't know, but I didn't think we were in immediate danger. "But we weren't aware of any sprite bloodlines either. We don't know if there are others, and I'm assuming they must be rare, or we would have."

"Then what is on that mountain, Cyrus?" Her voice wavered.

"There is only one way to find out."

Drew walked a zigzag line back to us, and I couldn't help but chuckle at his playfulness.

"Let's go," he said. His enthusiasm was hard to ignore.

"He's not afraid." I winked at Leana to try to lighten the weight on her.

"He's not seen enough of the world to know to be."

"I'm not afraid. I want to climb the mountain." Drew held both arms up in the air. "Time to go."

I shifted to my fae form and held my hand out to him. Seeing how eager and relaxed he was made it hard to be on edge. He seemed to be more excited the closer we got, and there was a certain comfort in witnessing the delight from him. "Come. Let's find out what's waiting for us."

"Whee," he said, tugging my hand. *And so, our journey begins.*

CHAPTER 9

THE CLIMB

Boulders and other debris littered the base of the mountain. I spotted tracks where they had recently fallen down the side. I didn't see signs of hoof prints, paw prints, or footprints from fae. For all intents and purposes, it looked as if nothing had disturbed this area in decades, maybe centuries, save some landslides. Other than natural events like erosion, the climb looked safe.

Leana tilted her head up to stare at the rough face. "What do you think?"

"I sense absolutely nothing here. Not a bird. Not an animal. No creatures. You?" The absence of life with the heavy burden of power threw me off-kilter, but the path ahead was our best option. Something drew me—us—to the spot we were now. The need to press on remained steady. I didn't know where it came from, but my assumption was that the Fates oversaw our actions for this journey. If I was wrong, I could be leading us into a trap, but despite not having a glimpse of the future, I knew I wasn't.

Leana shook her shoulders like she could shake off the weight in the air. "Not one living thing other than the flora. Do you think it could be magic—like our glamour?"

"That's what I'm thinking, but it feels solid." I tapped my fist against the side of the mountain.

"So, do you think it's safe?"

"Up." Drew pointed and jumped. His confirmation was the only answer that seemed to matter, because I wanted to climb too. Normally, I wouldn't trust a child's instinct so easily on something so dangerous, but that sense of calling and needing to know intensified in my chest.

"We knew there were risks when we decided to make this trip."

"That was when I thought no life resided on this mountain." She looked down at Drew. "Cyrus, if something happens, and it's between me and Drew, you choose Drew. Promise me."

I didn't want to make that promise, but I felt I owed it to her for what I'd put her through the last five years... maybe longer. If it had been Gemma in this situation, I would have given my life for my charge long before our bonding ceremony, so I understood her request. "You know what you ask of me?"

She nodded. "I do. No matter what, he lives."

"I will promise you I will do what it takes to make sure he stays alive."

"Thank you." She let out a breath and shifted into her natural form. "Now, let's climb."

I placed Drew on her back. "Remember how tight you held on yesterday?"

He smiled and nodded.

"Hold on even tighter today."

"Yes, Cyrus," he said. He'd never used my name before that I could recall, and the progress reminded me of his trauma. My heart tightened in my chest for what he'd seen at a young age—his mother's death, his oldest sister's disappearance, his other sister's kidnapping, and the only home he'd ever known collapse when the magic of the prison kingdom flickered out.

"You will be fine." I let my glamour go into my unicorn form. Climbing the rough landscape was easier in my natural state.

"I know," he said.

I snorted and laughed. "Good. Time to climb."

I led the way as we navigated the steep terrain. It would take us most of the day to reach the valley, and I hoped I could get us there before the sun set. It would be close, and if we had to backtrack at any point, we wouldn't make it. My hooves connected to the surface, and there was power in the soil but nothing concealed. Boulders and rocks of various sizes littered the face, and we had to pick through them on slick grass. The sun approached midday, and the warmth heated my skin. I hoped it would dry some of the dew from the ground to make the climb easier.

"If you sense anything, send it down the bond. I'll leave it open for you."

"You didn't close it after last night?" Concerned etched her voice.

"No." I glanced back at her. She'd stopped.

"I didn't hear any of your thoughts, and you didn't meld into my dreams."

Shock sent a cold chill down my spine. "Try to send something to me."

Her mouth fell open. "I am."

Nothing. No sweet tinkling musical words or angry or tired or any of those sounds bounced around in my head. The magic in these lands must dampen ours, and that could be a problem if it came to a fight. We were both trained in non-magical combat, but damn if it wasn't easier with magic. "I'm getting nothing. Let me try to open more."

Leana looked rooted in place. I turned inward, pulling a few more stones out of my mental wall.

"Try now."

"I haven't stopped."

What the fuck. I mentally yelled since that didn't seem appropriate language for Drew.

"Did you just whisper profanity?"

"No, I screamed it in my mind. But you heard that?"

"It was so soft that if I hadn't been listening, I might not have heard it," she said, her tone edgy and nervous.

"So, we're dampened here, but my magic still feels strong."

"As does mine," Leana said. "Should we try something?"

"We can't in front of the boy." One of the few laws we

were bound to meant keeping our real magic a secret. It would only make us bigger targets with the vampires and others.

"But how will we know if we can defend ourselves in a fight?"

I took a step forward and motioned for them to follow. "We have power beyond our magic."

Leana studied me for several moments. She appeared to be listening as if she could hear the magic in the earth. She took a few tentative steps. "I don't like this, Cyrus."

"We all dislike the unknown. It is our nature." The ground rumbled as if in answer. I tilted my head up. Pebbles fell toward us. Behind the tiny rocks were several large boulders. *Fucking gods.* I shifted to my human form and pushed Leana and Drew out of the path.

Leana screamed, changing form in the air, and wrapping her human arms around Drew to cushion the impact of their fall.

Cyrus. I heard her voice in my head and pivoted. A giant boulder rolled straight for me. Leana and Drew were at my back. I had seconds to decide. My choices were limited, so I exposed my horn and lowered my head to meet the giant rock. It shattered into thousands of pieces. My head pounded, and I dropped to my knees. If I'd shifted back to my natural state, the impact wouldn't have been as bad. I only had time to get my horn out, and that left me vulnerable in my faelike appearance. I wouldn't be able to return to my true form until my body restored itself. The pull of sleep beckoned like a lullaby.

Leana came to my side. "Let me help."

"You know you cannot. Only time and rest will." I debated whether to lead us back down the mountain to try again tomorrow or to push forward. If we pushed forward, I would slow us down in my state. Sprites were known for tests and traps, so we could face this same situation again tomorrow. The more I forced my aching head and neck to think through the little information I knew about the sprites, the more I thought this was a test of perseverance and worthiness. In that case, moving forward, even slowly, was the better option.

"Then we go back," Leana said, looking down the way we came.

Drew, however, stared in the opposite direction. He raised his arm and pointed. "Me."

"We're not turning around. We're pushing forward."

She scrutinized me with a piercing stare as if she mentally dissected my insides. After what felt like an eternity under her harsh gaze, she extended a faelike hand toward me. I slipped mine into hers, and she helped me to my feet. The throb at the top of my head and the base of my skull intensified. I steadied myself and rubbed my temples. My body longed for the rest it would be denied for now.

"I only do this because I trust you, Cyrus."

"Thank you." I took several deep breaths to attempt to calm my throbbing head. It would only get worse until I rested, but for now, we'd continue our ascent.

CHAPTER 10

THE GUESTS

I leaned over behind a large boulder, hidden from Leana's and Drew's view, and retched. I heaved until nothing was left in my stomach. My head ached like I'd been kicked over and over again, making it hard to think. The pain impaired my decision-making skills. I was a liability and good to no one. If whatever was on the mountain wanted to attack, I wouldn't be able to fight them off. The only thought that repeated in my head was of sleep.

When I emerged, Leana looked me over. Pity and something else I couldn't determine marked her features. "We can stop here and finish in the morning."

The sun approached dusk. While we could see in the dark, it did present a risk. I gauged the distance, and we had another hour at least. We had a small chance to make the rise before dark. Slim but possible. The remainder was steep, and I hoped it would reveal the edge of the valley. If we could just get there, that would be good for the night.

My senses were telling me that, and I'd trusted them. "I think we try it."

My body revolted against the idea. Agony radiated from the top of my head and pulsed in stabbing throbs through my neck and down my spine to my tailbone. Every step was like fighting in a battle with no end in sight, but there was an end here. I just had to get to the spot.

Leana sighed. "Drew, do you want to camp here—"

Drew pointed up before she could finish the options. "Me."

"Looks like I'm overruled."

THE SUN DROPPED below the ridgeline when we reached the edge of the valley. The climb down, nearly as steep as the climb up, would be a slow descent. I relaxed, beyond ready to give in to the rest my body demanded and have a break from the misery. "We'll make that trek tomorrow."

Drew danced around Leana like he attended a celebration. She looked worried, and I understood why. The space felt safe, but that could be a trick. The pain could have made me more malleable. While I didn't think there was cause to be concerned, I didn't trust how my brain was working with the distraction either.

"He seems happy with the choice at least."

"It's beautiful," she said, taking in the view.

The colors were breathtaking, and I soaked them up

before the last bits of sunlight disappeared. Leana and I stood in silence as Drew continued his party.

"I'll make a fire."

Leana presented in her human form, covering my hand with hers. "You should rest. I can make the fire. I'm pretty good at it now."

I nodded and sat on the ground, fighting the appeal of sleep while she went to work. Drew followed me and sat in my lap. I wasn't sure if he mirrored my actions, felt cold, or felt safe with me. "Are you okay?"

He patted my cheek, and I took that to mean yes.

"It's okay to go with Leana if you want to." I was happy he'd warmed up to me, but I was in no shape to take care of him. Exhaustion threatened to take over any second.

"No, I'll stay with you."

Leana piled up the wood and snapped her fingers to start the flame for the fire. The warmth beckoned the drowsiness to take over, and I fought giving in to it until Leana was settled and could watch Drew.

"You can sleep, Cyrus," Leana said. "I'm awake, and I'll rouse you if anything happens."

"I made you a promise," I said, my speech slurred. My eyes were so heavy, they drooped, making it almost impossible to keep them open. I tried again. "I made you a promise."

"And you will keep it if you need to. I don't think you do right now, so sleep."

I woke with a jolt. Gemma filled my dreams, and I hadn't realized my dreams had been empty since I left her—shut her out of our bond. But Laurel was there too. We were all in a lush, green field. Laurel and I held our hands up, fingers entwined, like a bridge. Gemma twirled with her daughter underneath. What seemed like thousands of small purple butterflies fluttered around us. A life that would never be faded away as dreams always did once I awoke. Letting go of sleep meant letting go of the illusion of a life with Gemma and Laurel. Warmth encircled me and comforted the agony that had suffocated my body. I'd pushed through for Leana and Drew, but it had taken its toll. I blinked my eyes open to the flickering fire Leana had set. She sat cross-legged in her fae form, holding Drew in her lap. Her arms were wrapped around him like a cocoon. They looked like a family, and I imagined Gemma similarly holding her daughter with Laurel sitting beside them. My eyes burned, and I blinked the images away.

I tested my faelike limbs, and while sore, I could move them without burning pain. My vision was a little blurry. I raised my hand to my head. A dull ache radiated where I touched, but the sheer throbbing from earlier had broken.

"How are you feeling?" Leana asked softly.

"Better," I said, swallowing against the thickness in my throat. "I think I can let the glamour go."

"Maybe hold off on that for a bit. We have guests." Her

voice was too calm, and I bolted up. A sharp pain throbbed in my skull from the movement, but I ignored it.

A flurry of light buzzed around us. A warm white ball shifted from side to side in front of my face. I shuffled away from it.

"Move slowly like you would with a wild animal. They are afraid of us."

"They?" I focused my gaze on the little bits of light and didn't trust what I was seeing. *I must have a concussion from the collision with the boulder.* "Are they sprites?"

"Yes." Leana kept her voice low. "They came not long after I lit the fire."

Godsdammit. I should have forced myself to stay awake. "Have they communicated?"

"No, I think they are investigating us. They are very interested in Drew. He fell asleep, so I guess his interest in them couldn't overcome his need for rest."

I chuckled. If enough time had passed that Drew fell asleep and nothing had happened, the sprites likely meant no harm to us. "After all the pointing and insistence."

"He is still a child, and it was a harrowing day for him."

"True." I noticed how many of them clustered around Drew. The little balls of light didn't dart around him like they had me, but the sprites stayed close to him as if they made a tiny wall of light to protect him. They were mostly focused on him while a few seemed to check out me and Leana. "Our lore depicts them as quite mischievous."

"I noticed when one braided my hair." She turned her

head to the side, and a perfect single braid cascaded over her shoulder.

"Looks good." I smiled.

"Thanks. Not very practical for our kind, though."

"That's a shame, because it does look pretty on you." Her cheeks pinkened.

I hadn't meant to embarrass her with the comment, but maybe it was something else. Shame sank it the pit of my stomach. I turned my head. A sprite floated right in front of me, and my vision had cleared enough that I could see the detail. While glowing like moonlight, a small ethereal body hovered at eye level. I believed it to be female.

"Can you communicate?" I asked, keeping my voice low like Leana.

The sprite's body began to stretch and morph. *Erebus save us.* I'd never seen sprites or their abilities, but I hadn't expected an adaptation for body type. I should have, though, given the stories of comingling. The sprite expanded in size until she grew to human proportions, taking on a female persona and attire similar to ours, as if mirroring us. She had flame-red hair that seemed to blow in non-existent wind, but nothing about her came across as threatening. Still, I was cautious, observing her every movement.

"My name is Cyrus," I said.

"I am Neala." She placed an ethereal hand over her collarbone, and the air shimmered around her movement.

My head throbbed. I rubbed my forehead, and the pain lessened. "I thought your people were no longer in this realm with us?"

Neala smirked. "We can move between this realm and the one you think of as the spiritual realm."

With Nyx and Erebus? Wouldn't my father have known that?

"So, you've been in the other all this time?" Leana asked.

"We have."

"Why come back now?" I wanted the sprite's attention back on me.

"Because of him." She looked at Drew and back to me. "He needs us. Your people need us."

We needed help. That part was true. I wasn't convinced it was sprite help we needed, and I wouldn't be until I heard what they had to offer.

"He is fae. We are not. Leana and I are—"

Neala's grin broadened. "Unicorns. We know. We can see you as your true form."

"You can?" I wasn't aware that anyone could see through our glamour, and that seemed like something Father would have shared. He'd been my primary point of reference for sprites, but that didn't mean he knew all about them. With this powerful magic, the sprites could have let him see what they wanted to and concealed what they didn't want to share.

"Did you expect everything to be handed down in stories after we departed?"

Even our history was debated among the elders, so it was foolish to assume I knew everything about the sprites from stories. "No, I did not."

I glanced at Leana. She'd probably been glamoured

since I'd been out, and while she could hold the human form longer than most, she couldn't hold it as long as my gift allowed. " I can take Drew so you can relax."

She passed the sleeping boy to me, and I held him in my arms. Drew didn't stir. Holding him made me nervous, like I might break him if I wasn't careful, but he was content. The flurry of sprites followed. Leana cast a worried glance my way and let her glamour go. She was stronger in this form, so if it came to a fight, she was ready. I expected her to stand up on Drew's behalf, but not mine.

Neala studied me, but her expression was unreadable. "You are different from the others of your kind. Even your twin."

I jerked my head up. "How do you know I have a twin?"

"Just because we are not here does not mean we do not listen."

I sized up the sprite, baffled by how much I'd learned that hadn't been in our lessons. "So, you've watched this world and the difficulties without intervention."

"We were not needed until now."

"Explain."

"You are much like your grandfather," the sprite said. "He remained skeptical but hopeful. He didn't fear crossing boundaries."

My paternal grandfather passed a century before the war, and I never met him. That must be who she spoke of. By the accounts of my father, my grandfather was a great unicorn, one of the longest to lead. Father never told any stories I'd interpreted as boundary-crossing. She must be mistaken on that point and that I was anything like him.

I checked Drew's breathing to make sure he slept still. He was at peace in the presence of the sprites. I could sense how calm he was above and beyond his restful state. "Is Drew one of you?"

"He is something more. An embodiment of this world, if you will."

"What do you mean?" Leana asked.

The sprite narrowed its eyes at her and came back to me. "He is part of us, part fae, part you, part human—all of this world."

"But not vampire?" Leana asked.

The sprite didn't look at her this time and directed the answer to me. "He is that, too, but not in the way you are used to with the nosferatu. He is...different."

Horseshit was how I interpreted what she shared. The likelihood seemed impossible and raised a thousand questions, but I settled on one to ask. "How is it possible that he can be all of these?

"It should not be, yet here he is."

Leana moved closer. "Did you call him here?"

"His heritage harkened him to the sacred land, and we heard his call."

"And you answered." I didn't ask the question but rather made a statement because the answer seemed obvious.

"We did. It's quite nice to be back in this realm, so we are pleased someone finally asked for our return."

Leana edged over next to me and Drew. "Do you need to be invited? I thought you could move on your own."

"We can, but we go where we are needed most."

I considered what the next step should be. Should I remain silent and let her elaborate, or was every piece of information going to be this push and pull?

"You want to know more." She smiled.

"Of course, but I'm not sure what else to ask."

"Perhaps the time for questions is done and the time for exploring is here." She held out her very human or fae-looking hand and gestured to the valley.

Drew stirred in my arms, blinking his sleepy eyes open. He scanned for and found Leana. He squirmed in my arms, so I set him down next to her. She remained in her natural form and positioned her body so that Drew was between us. The protective stance didn't stop the sprites from buzzing around to get close to him. Drew laughed and reached for them as they moved back and forth. He'd made friends, but the warrior in me needed a verbal confirmation.

"Is it safe for us? All of us?" I asked.

"As safe as anywhere in this realm."

I glanced at Leana. She gave a nod of her head.

"Will you be going with us?"

"I will be. The others will be around." She smiled again, and her teeth seemed to elongate and then shrink back—almost like she struggled to keep this form. I wondered if it was similar to how other unicorns glamoured between their human-like or faelike forms. Because the sprite spoke the truth. I was different from the others in that aspect. As long as I wasn't injured, I could hold my alternate persona as long as I wanted without draining my power or needing to recover. Marius didn't even have that gift. He had others, but not that one. We were twins, but not identical in every way like those few before us.

I reached for Drew's hand, and he placed his tiny fingers in mine. Leana stood in her natural form on his other side, and with pre-dawn light, we began the descent into the valley.

CHAPTER II
IMPOSSIBLE

Bright-tinted foliage covered the fields, visible even in the dim light. The flowers and leaves changed shades as the sprites, in their winged, tiny forms, brushed their fingertips against them. Unicorns had certain elemental magic similar to fae, and some could alter the hue of vegetation. The effortless action of the sprites was the remarkable difference. It almost seemed like a connection to the essences, as if the colors were manifestations of their magic.

I followed what looked like a path toward the center of the valley. The sprite didn't correct my direction, so I assumed I ventured the right way. Drew's excitement increased from giggles to dancing the deeper we went and gave me further confirmation. My senses weren't giving off any unusual vibes, so it felt...safe. I still worried, because safety wasn't something we had been used to in the last two hundred years. Comfortable? Yes. Safe? No.

The early dawn light began to break over the mountain peaks and cast a pinkish-orange hue over the valley. The sprites, except for the one next to me, darted up, spinning into it as if soaking up the warmth or light. Drew tilted his head up, watching and clapping.

"Do you want to join them?" I cut my gaze over to Neala.

"There will be other times. My task today is as your guide."

"Not much guiding happening."

She laughed; it tinkled like the high-pitched noise that shattered crystal. "Am I not? Have I not answered your questions and shown you the path?"

"Hmmm," I said, skeptical that we were being directed anywhere specific.

Leana huffed, echoing my sentiment. "You could tell us more about this area and what we are walking into."

The sprite flashed a smile filled with warmth, like the sun the others were busy enjoying. "Some things are better to be seen than to be explained."

She made a hard argument for me to refute. There were things I'd viewed in my lifetime that I could never explain deeply enough to convey the beauty. One of those moments being the exquisite look on Gemma's face when she'd used her wind power to shield an attack for the first time after the bonding ceremony. We were training, and I threw a flurry of ground and water at her. She held everything at bay without a drop getting on her. The proud smile on her face had stolen my breath. I pushed that thought quickly away. Getting emotional here was the last thing that needed to happen.

"I think you both know something of how painful seeing the truth can be," Neala said, her voice a bit sad. "But not from the same events."

I glanced at Leana and instantly regretted it. She wore a mass of mixed emotions on her face. While I couldn't read them all, I could feel them down the weak bond I'd left open for her to reach me. The connection was less inhibited, perhaps from the sprite's presence or doing. Leana's features portrayed love and pain and joy and sadness, and I didn't suppress them. I deserved her pain. It was mine to bear.

"Don't," she whispered, turning her head away from me.

I trained my gaze down to the damp grass we had trodden on and inhaled the safe scent. There were worse places to be than here in this moment, and I deserved them all.

"You are hard on yourself, unicorn," the sprite said.

Not hard enough for the pain I inflicted. "My decisions have caused injury to those I care for, so I should be."

"You are better than you give yourself credit for. You have walked a path most cannot." Her choice of words overwhelmed me...like she saw into my soul.

"I have walked a different path than most unicorns, but that doesn't make me better than what I believe I am." A bonded guard should be a source of strength, but I'd almost broken Gemma when I left. I wasn't supposed to hurt her. My oath bound me to protect her. The dishonor of my actions shuddered through me.

"She knows why you left," the sprite said in a gentle voice.

I wasn't sure if she meant Gemma or Leana, but it was almost as if she could read my thoughts. *Son of a bitch.* I built my wall back up. With Leana in my sight, I could keep it up, and I'd tear it down if we got separated. For now, I had to get the sprite out of my head.

"That only works with your kind." The sprite's lips quirked up.

"What only works with our kind?" Leana asked.

"Your...what do you call it? Paired match? He has attempted to block me from his thoughts."

Fucking bloody gods.

Leana's eyes widened. "You can read our thoughts?"

"Only when I choose to. Your paired match has had a troubled and unusual life."

I was more than a paired match and so was Leana. The sprite's use of the reference for our relationship probably brought Leana pain.

She held the emotion in if it had. Instead, Leana nuzzled Drew's head. He kicked a rock ahead of us.

"I see your distress, too, Leana," the sprite said. "But I see great love for you soon."

If the sprite meant me, she'd made up a complete fabrication. I hoped that Leana would find real adoration, and my fondest wish was for her to find a sincere devotion. A tingle bit against my arm, and I saw the sprite's hand there. She studied me, but her face masked her reaction. *What is she looking for from me?* "You will have great love too."

Not being able to block her from my thoughts unnerved me. I wanted the sprite out of my head. The intrusion and lack of privacy was the same reason I avoided the collective. I didn't want to have this conversation, and the only result would be more pain for Leana, and I refused to be the cause. I wandered ahead of them, but the sprite followed while Leana hung back with Drew.

"You put all others above yourself. Do you see that?" the sprite asked me.

"I believe that is the first wrong thing you have said." I wasn't putting anyone above me when I fell in love with and fucked my bonded and her mate.

The sprite laughed that high, tinkling sound again. "It is not wrong just because you don't see it. I think that makes it even more correct."

"You know what I did. How can you say that?"

"The perception you are holding close to your heart is flawed. She loves you. He loves you. Their daughter is your daughter too."

My breath lodged in my chest. *Impossible.* I froze on my last step. "What do you mean?"

"She is theirs. That is true. But your magic is mixed with the child's. You are part of her forever."

No way that could be true. It wasn't possible. "How can that be?"

"Your tears, like the rest of you, are different. The magic will never wane in the child. As long as she lives, she will carry a part of you."

My chest clenched. I'd never given a tear to anyone,

unicorn or fae, before the one I gave Gemma to save baby Daphina. "Is it like a bond with the fae? I haven't felt her."

"It is not, but she is young and this is new. Who knows what it will be like when she matures?"

"Something tells me you know exactly how it will be."

The sprite just smiled and strolled forward. "Not everything needs to be known."

CHAPTER 12

THE CIRCLE

Coming to the mountain, to the meadow, was a mistake. Neala's actions convinced me the sprite fed off my torture—maybe Leana's too.

"Do not fret, unicorn. You are safe here, as are your companions."

I plodded forward, positioning myself between the sprite and the others. "It doesn't feel that way when you are tormenting us."

Neala's face contorted into surprise—at least that's what I thought the awkward expression meant. "Is that how you receive good news from others? I think it must be."

"What good news have you shared with us...or any real news at all?" I grumbled more to myself but didn't care if the sprite heard me.

"You offend me. I've imparted much more to you than is necessary and much more than I should have because I like you."

I stopped. Laughter roared out of my mouth like I'd never experienced. I bent over at the waist and slapped my knee. It felt good to let something out with everything so pent up in me. I straightened and held my sides. I caught a glimpse of Leana and Drew. Concern etched Leana's delicate features, and Drew's brows pinched together.

The sprite eyed me as if she wanted to smack me, but she didn't move. "Are you quite done with your display?"

"I am." One last chuckle escaped me as I straightened to my full height.

"Good. Then your ungrateful ass might notice that we are here."

I took in our surroundings. We'd made it to the center of the valley. All the sprites seemed to have gravitated to an area surrounded by stones. They were set similar to the position of numbers on one of the fae clocks. "What are we supposed to see?"

"What you wish to see."

Sprites were known for trickery far more than fae. Although the fae took frequent blame from the humans. "And the catch is?"

"No catch, as you put it. This is for the child to find peace, but you and the other unicorn may find it useful as well."

Not one part of me would let Drew or Leana do anything with whatever the sprite showed us until I tested it out first. Leana scooted in behind me with Drew, and I wished I could let my mental wall down to speak to her without the sprite hearing us.

"What are we supposed to do?"

"Step into the center and see what it is time to show you," she said, her tone empathetic and kind. The way she said it was as if I should already know the answers it would show me.

"Me first." Drew laughed, running toward the circle. I dove for him and caught the blur of Leana reaching for him from my periphery. He seemed to speed up, and neither of us was fast enough.

"No," Leana and I yelled in unison.

The circle lit up with light like the sprites, and Drew moved in slow motion. My heart sped up. I had to get him out. Then the little boy just froze.

I tried to break the barrier with my magic, but the sprite pulled me back with hers. My struggle against her was overpowered by her magical strength.

Leana screamed. Multiple sprites held her at the legs and neck. "Let me go."

"Let us both go." I shifted into my unicorn form, ready to use my horn, if necessary, but the sprite's power was greater than I anticipated. She held a hand up toward me, creating a magical wall and successfully pushing me back from the circle. The pattern, visible to me now, was intricate and wouldn't be broken easily.

"I assure you, Drew is not harmed. He's connecting."

"Connecting with what?" All I saw was light and an unmoving Drew. If they hurt him...or worse, I wouldn't stop until they were all wiped from the realm, and I didn't care if the sprite heard my thoughts.

Neala sighed and shook her head. "You will see."

A young woman, spritely in form, appeared as if she

walked through a door in front of Drew. She looked familiar, from her white-blonde hair to her delicate frame, but I'd never met a sprite before today. Her youthful features came into focus. I couldn't believe what I was seeing. She'd been the bride Albert took after General Daphina died. *Sion. Drew's Mother.*

"Mommy!" Drew's voice danced across the circle in a normal cadence despite the way his body floated—suspended in the space. He'd been a babe when she died and couldn't remember her. But he did.

"How can this be?"

"You know that we can travel to the spirit realm and other realms. Why would this not be possible?"

"Andrews," she said, taking ethereal steps toward the boy. "I've missed you. I'm so glad you remember me."

"I see you at night when my eyes are closed."

"Ahh, yes, your dreams. I visit you there when I can."

Drew hadn't been able to tell anyone that when he wasn't speaking. He'd carried his mother's visits inside him, and I understood the toll of keeping a secret so big. I hurt for him to have dealt with that at such a young age. I studied Leana. Tears welled in her eyes. This was not the place to spill them. The sight kicked my instincts back on. I gave her one shake of my head. She met my gaze and closed her eyes tightly. I turned back to the circle and stopped struggling.

"I need to tell you some things, and although you are young, I need you to remember them for one day when they matter. We might not get this chance again."

I witnessed a mother giving her son closure, something I never had with my parents. My heart pounded.

"Yes, Mommy." Drew nodded his head in slow motion, but his voice came out at normal speed.

"You are a very special boy," she said, kneeling to be eye-to-eye with him. "One day, you will be very important in this world, and when that time comes, you will need to be very brave."

"I'm brave." A slow smile spread across his face.

My heart warmed seeing him proud and having a moment with his mother he never got in this realm. The beauty of the moment far outweighed my struggles getting us here. It was worth every bit of the pain I'd endured.

She smiled in return. "Yes, you are, but when this day comes, and you will know the day, you will have to be extra brave for not just yourself but everyone."

"I promise to always be brave, Mommy."

Magic hummed in the air around us. He'd made a promise, and the oath coursed in him like his blood. Those promises often backfired for many of the creatures of this world, particularly fae and unicorn. My gut twisted, but I hoped it wouldn't be the case for him.

She pressed a hand over his heart. "While you are being so brave, I want you to remember that Mommy loved you with everything she had to give."

She turned into little sparks of light—magic. She absorbed into Drew where she touched him. Love, pure and absolute, diffused the air around us with comfort akin to a hug. I worked on a swallow as I lived Drew's joy with him, watching him receive a final gift from a mother to a son. We all bore witness to something we'd likely never see again in our lifetimes.

"Mommy?" Drew called in a bewildered voice. His movements returned to normal, and he looked at Leana. His mouth turned down, and his amber gaze darted around in confusion.

Leana shifted into her fae form, and he ran toward her. She scooped him up in her arms. "I'm always here for you, Drew. I accept you as my charge."

Magic crackled in the air for a second time, and this time it sealed their bond. I knew firsthand the pain and happiness of that bond for a unicorn. Our magic, albeit a small sliver, forever left our souls to join with the charge for their lifetime. It only returned to us after the charge left the realm—one significant aspect that set it apart from a mate bond. I remembered how resentful I'd been that the Fates wanted me to give up a piece of magic and how insignificant that felt when the promise to protect snapped into place. Protection was guaranteed by all unicorns, but the responsibility was that of the bonded. The bonding ceremony would follow later when Drew reached an age old enough to accept what Leana offered, but for now, he would be under unicorn protection.

"Maybe you don't need the circle after all." The sprite gave Leana an approving gaze.

"There are no questions I need answered," Leana replied with confidence.

"You feel unfortunate in many ways, but I promise

there is some goodness in your future." The sentiment was probably the kindest thing the sprite had said.

Leana took a step backward. "That's more than I need to know. I prefer to experience my life and not anticipate it."

The sprite bowed her head to Leana. "As you wish." She turned to me. "Then that leaves you, grumpy unicorn."

Leana giggled.

The last thing I wanted was my personal journey to be displayed three-dimensionally for everyone to see. I wasn't frightened of the circle, but I was afraid for the pain Leana might experience from what was brought forth for me. "I'm not sure I need anything from the circle either."

"Oh, but I must insist this time." The sprite gave me a shove hard enough to push me across the boundary and into the circle.

The space pulsed with old and heavy magic and forced me into my faelike form. Moving my limbs was like flailing through the quicksand that could be found in the Forgotten Forest. Light danced around me. A buffer prevented the sounds from entering the circle. Turning my head to look for Leana wouldn't work. We'd be here all night waiting for that kind of movement. *Fuck it. Drew is fine. It can't be that bad.*

I opened myself to the ancient power. The white light enveloped the space until I could see nothing else. No one walked through an invisible door to greet me. Instead, a force thrust me through a supernatural wall like I was vanyshened by a fae, only my body seemed weightless as it moved through time and space. The feeling was reminiscent of my near-death experience on the battlefield, and I tried to ignore the way it suffocated me.

Then, the love of my heart appeared there with her mate. Gemma's golden-red hair obscured her face, and Laurel's head was turned toward her. I drifted closer, shocked their eyes were barely open. Strange purple marks marred their perfect faces. My chest seized and tightened. Chains bound them to a wall. More black and bluish discolorations tainted the skin on their arms.

Both had been beaten until they were almost unrecognizable. Anger raged in me. I reached out to free them from their bonds, but I had nobody to take action. Their bodies sagged as if they couldn't support their weight. I knew well the weary and weak expression on the black and blue faces of Gemma and Laurel. I'd memorized that same expression as I'd inflicted punishment on vampires —tortured during the war to find out who led them. The two most important fae to me hung on a wall, exhausted from repetitive abuse. Damn the consequences, I tried my magic, and it didn't respond either. *What is this? Where are they? How do I get to them?*

Albert walked into view, flanked by a dozen vampire soldiers. My fury amplified at the sight of the false king. I would pierce him with my horn and enjoy watching his body explode. Then I'd put him back together and do it again until I saw that he felt every ounce of agony times ten that he'd inflicted on Gemma and Laurel. *Their daughter. Where was she?* Panic pulsated through my soul. I scanned as much of the area as I could for Phina, but I didn't see any trace of her. Her absence brought some relief. I prayed to our ancestors and the fae's goddesses and gods that she remained far away from this place.

Gemma? Can you hear me? I reached down our bond. It'd been so long since we'd communicated. Would she even answer if she could?

Suffering like I'd experienced as a soldier in the war strangled me. It was worse than I thought, and I fought for purchase where I had none. I couldn't physically get to them, and it was breaking me. Gemma looked up at Albert, who stood in front of where I...wherever I was.

If you can hear me, I'm coming for you—for you both.

She scrutinized the space just above her father. I was sure she could see me but then her gaze cut to the left and right. *Cyrus, is it really...*Her thought paused on the bond. *I hear you. Don't come. There are too many of them. Get Phina from the palace and make sure she's safe and find Drew. They are the future. Keep them as far away from my father as you can.*

She came through loud and strong, even though she must be some distance away. That was my Gemma, her strength winning out over the excruciating pain she must be in. I'd tell her what a warrior she was in her own right when I saw her in person, because nothing could keep me away from her and Laurel. *I have Drew, and I'll get Phina.*

She closed her eyes. *Thank you.*

Then I'm coming to free you and Laurel. And kill Albert, but I didn't need to share that part with her.

He wants to drain our power.

Fight. I'll be there as quickly as I can. And Gemma?

She opened her bruised and swollen eyes, and I could see the brutal agony.

I love you. I love you both. I'd missed them both so much and letting her know like this wasn't the way it should have happened. Regret ripped at my heart, but I'd make it up to them.

Love mixed with relief slid down the bond like snow melting on a sunny day. *I love you too, and I know Laurel would say the same.*

She was the sun and Laurel the blue sky, and they were mine. *Don't give up. I promise I'm coming.*

Magic zinged around me for the promise, and I broke the connection with her. The thickness of the circle dissipated, and my limbs moved freely. A little purple butterfly flitted in front of me as if it came to confirm the choices made at the circle.

"Now you know what you must do," the sprite said.

"I do. My promise has been given freely and will be kept." I turned toward Leana, assuming she and the others saw what I did.

"I'm coming with you. I go where Drew goes," Leana said.

I knew as soon as I made the promise what it meant. My promise and hers were intertwined in destiny, and I knew that would end in pain for both of us. I'd pay the price with my life to save those I loved.

PART TWO
SUNRISE & SUNSET

From the Unicorn Archives passed down through the leaders to the historians.

A prophecy was told from the sprites to the unicorns of a day when the realm would be much changed. The leaders of all kinds would find themselves at a crossroads on the survival of the realm—one choice would allow magic to live on, and the other would usher in a new era. Should the path without magic be chosen, many would not survive. Entire species would cease to be. The world remaining would forget the power that once lived in the lands and beings who possessed it. The seer who foretold the prophecy said Nyx would weep for the loss of her children but would not interfere with the decisions of those entrusted to make them. When the day dawned, she would not take away the freewill once taken from her, even if it meant magic died with the sunset.

CHAPTER 13

PATIENCE

Leana and I ran at a speed most unicorns couldn't maintain. She held Drew in place for so long that her magic must be drained, though she acted as if it wasn't. In fact, her stamina held strong. Still, I worried for the boy. At his young age, he needed breaks. I'd prefer to push through rather than lose the time, but I couldn't do that to a child, especially one with unicorn protection. My promise to Gemma hummed around me.

"There's a creek up ahead. We can rest nearby and take care of Drew's needs."

"That's a good idea. I can tell he's tired."

I glanced toward where he sat on Leana's back. Drew's eyes were half-lidded. "He appears to be sleepy."

She smiled. "He has always been able to sleep anywhere. It's the staying asleep part that is hard for him."

I nodded. That trait ran in their family. Gemma and Arianna had both suffered from the inability to sleep at times. My memory flashed to the state I'd seen Gemma in, and my chest contracted. *Erebus, I'm not known for my patience, but I could use some right now.*

Drew jerked awake and sat up straight.

"We're going to stop here for a bit," I said, lifting him and setting him on his feet. He took off running to the water.

"We do have canteens," Leana called after him.

Drew flopped onto his knees, scooping water with his hands.

"Perhaps we should take more frequent breaks," I said, watching the small boy guzzle water. We had to get to Phina quickly. The time sacrifice wasn't something I wanted to give up, but I would to make the trip easier for Drew.

"It looks that way. I've never seen him so thirsty," Leana said, walking toward him. He took off running behind a tree before she could get to him. A laugh rumbled through my chest, and I let it go. She glamoured into her fae form and put her hands on her hips.

I came to stand beside her.

"Cyrus," she said, keeping her voice low. "I know you carry much guilt for what happened, but you shouldn't. Not just because I asked Marius for the pairing, but because I, too, had a lover. I waited for years and only recently allowed myself to explore the relationship. Maybe not like you do for Gemma, but I care for him."

Her admission surprised me. Happiness followed. Leana didn't owe me an explanation, but I wondered why she chose this moment to share the details. She deserved to experience the intense love like I had for Gemma. No resentment stirred in me for her choice, nor did I see it as a betrayal. "I told you before I wanted you to be happy, and the sprite said a great love is in your future. My earnest wish for you is that it comes to be."

"I hope you mean that."

"Of course, I do."

She wrung her faelike hands. "Because I believe I am… pregnant."

Fear twisted my gut at the thought it could be mine, but it couldn't be. The life in her grew from half her and half her lover, and it was a blessing from Erebus she conceived. "Congratulations. Life is a beautiful miracle, and I am happy for you."

"You're not going to kill him, are you?"

I smirked. "No, I'll keep my horn to myself. Unless he doesn't want to raise the babe with you. Then, I might have to threaten him."

Her cheeks in fae form had been rosier. A smile softened the apprehension on her face. "He wants to raise our creation together. It was all new. I haven't been with anyone else. I suspected but didn't know for sure until after you arrived, or I would have told you that first day."

"So, it is someone from the encampment?"

"Yes, but we knew each other before and became closer after we left the prison kingdom."

I gave her shoulder a gentle squeeze. Of course, I wanted to know who, but I wouldn't pressure her to tell. "You do not need to explain to me. I mean it when I say I hope this is the great love the sprite spoke of for you.

What about proclaiming Drew as your charge and having a new unicorn at the same time? Two younglings together will be hard. How do you feel about that?"

"Drew is still young. It will be a year before this one"—she rubbed her stomach—"will be here. By the time Drew is ready to formalize our bond, my youngling will be old enough to start training as well."

Drew came running toward us with his hands out. The days of this carefree joy would pass all too quickly for him, and destiny would come calling.

Leana picked him up. "Are you hungry? I bet you are ready for a snack."

"Chocolate!" Drew clapped his hands together.

"Let's eat some fruit first," she said with a laugh.

"I like fruit too," he said but with far less enthusiasm.

"I'm going to patrol to make sure there are no issues." Nothing had stood out as a threat, but I didn't want to take any chances while we weren't moving. With Albert after power his own children and grandchild, I wouldn't put it past him to send vampires into the fae lands.

Leana nodded. I didn't want to leave them alone, but I needed a minute. I wasn't lying when I wished her happiness, but loss still languidly looped through my gut. Everything that had once been between us came to an end. Leana would move on with her new family, and I hoped Gemma and Laurel would take me back so we could build our lives together. Gemma had said they both loved me, but loving someone didn't mean they could be in a relationship.

Drew would connect Leana and me in another way

than we were used to, so we would see each other, but things would be different. Once the announcement of our split and her pregnancy became public, the need to keep appearances would end. Several centuries ago, news like ours would have been scandalous, but those times had mostly passed. I suspected my situation, a unicorn with not one but two fae, would draw a little more scrutiny given our reproduction situation.

MY LIMBS EXTENDED into four legs, and the soft dirt gave under my hooves. With the news Leana shared, I wished I'd brought Cleave along or at least one of the others. She would have insisted on making the trip regardless because of her commitment to Drew. Births for our kind were so rare these days. With my handful of nieces and nephews scattered around the realm as proof, Marius had been the only male unicorn capable of producing any heirs, but this couldn't be his. He hadn't been here, and she wouldn't have been able to contact him. It wasn't his. I didn't want to put any additional stress on her. If she hadn't volunteered the information about who fathered this miracle, I'd ask her later, when we were settled in the fae court.

I wandered back to where Leana and Drew sat. Drew made little glints of light with his fingers, similar to the light of the sprites. I glamoured to my faelike form and leaned against a tree. Leana was going to make a wonderful mother and role model. She looked up and smiled as if she heard my thoughts, but I'd closed off the bond between us. The sun glided past the peak of the day, and I was eager to get us back on the move.

"Ready? We could make it by nightfall."

"We're ready. Aren't we, Drew?"

"There's a baby in your belly." He reached out and placed a hand on her stomach.

His proclamation stunned me. There were only a few unicorn and far fewer fae who could sense conception. I straightened. Had Leana told him? Surely not so soon. Many things could go wrong, given she just confirmed the pregnancy. After the early months, the unicorn's scent became more pronounced, and others could tell.

"How do you know that?" she asked Drew, confirming my suspicion that she hadn't shared the news.

He shrugged. "The baby is happy."

"What makes you say that?"

"The baby told me, Leana." He looked at her like she should know.

Impressive gift if he was hearing the baby. I squatted down next to them. "I think he might be hearing the unicorn's thoughts in the same way the sprite heard mine and yours."

"Are you hearing the baby, Drew?" Leana asked.

He scrunched up his face. "Yes."

"That's going to make it harder to tell the news on your terms."

"It is, but it's a gift that he can share that connection."

"I've never heard of that kind of communication in the womb. It's quite impressive."

Drew's facial expression shifted. He looked perplexed.

"He'll need to be taught how to handle those messages coming to him, Leana."

Her mouth turned into a grim smile. "It will be overwhelming. I should be able to shield him somewhat with my magic, but his power grows every day. I'm not sure how long that will last."

She'd need her magic for the baby. I'd seen some of the dampening equipment the fae had, mostly confiscated from the vampires, but it could prove useful to ease Drew into this powerful gift.

"When we get to the fae court, they have some technology that might help."

She made a sour face. "I've heard of some of capabilities from others. I'm not a fan of it, but I want him to feel safe and be able to learn with other children without being made to feel different."

"I'm not sure there is much you can do to stop that. He is never going to be like the other children. The sprite told us he is special. That's a declaration of destiny and cannot be undone."

"No, it can't, but I'll still do my best to protect him."

"As you should with your charge, and you will have strong fae and unicorns standing with you to do so."

"Thank you." Leana rested her hand on my back. "You didn't have to come back. You didn't have to stay with us when I told you the truth about our pairing, my pregnancy, or when the sprite told us of Drew's heritage."

"You do not need to thank me, Leana. This is my duty, but even if it wasn't, I'd be here."

"I know you would, Cyrus, because you are good even when you don't see it." She turned to Drew with a bright smile. "Ready?"

"Time to go," Drew said.

"Yes, little man. Time to go." I lifted him onto Leana's back, so we could make the final leg of our journey to the fae court. Returning to the place I last saw Gemma was where I needed to be to fulfill my promise. As hard as it was to relive those memories, it was the images of Gemma and Laurel's imprisonment that threatened to crack my chest and nearly buckled my knees. I breathed through the visions of them suffering as I thought...*one step closer to saving Gemma and Laurel.*

CHAPTER 14
SEMANTICS

Casimir greeted us on the outskirts of the court. Marius had reached her before I could. I'd let my mental wall down for the run, but I put it back up when Casimir came into sight outside the fence of the court palace. She'd claimed the fae court as her area after so many years here by the side of the current prince. Her white coat glimmered like silk in the sunlight, and as beautiful as her coat was, she wore a scowl on her face, the complete opposite.

"You're not with Rainier?" Leana asked.

She didn't know the nature of the freedom Casimir and the prince afforded each other. However, her being at the gate made me curious who was with Phina.

"He is at the border of the vampire kingdom where he is needed." She turned to me with fire in her eyes. "Figuring out how to save your charge you abandoned."

Her words sank into my gut like a punch and nearly

doubled me over. All the guilt from my choices boiled the bile in my stomach and burned my throat.

"Seems you've done the same," Leana said in my defense before I could answer Casimir for myself.

"My charge and her mate are why I am here," I said, filling my tone with power and leveling my gaze on Marius's love, even if he never acknowledged it to the collective. Of course, as hateful as she was, I'm not sure I would either.

"Hmmph. If you hadn't left her, she might not be in this situation with the false fae king."

"Albert would have found a way, Casimir. Marius knew. Hell, we all understood nothing would stop Albert from coming after the power in Gemma and Arianna once he gained his freedom."

"It's not General Daphina's power or her daughters' he will get if he succeeds. It's Nyx's power, and he'll be unstoppable if he can drain them of such a force."

"I'm fully aware of what he's after and what the cost would be."

"Their line would die, Cyrus, and the last of Nyx's presence in this world with them." Casimir's venomous tone bit the air with a charge of magic.

My agitation returned the magic challenge. I waited for her next move.

Leana's eyes widened. General Daphina's lineage wasn't well known among all unicorns. The elders and Marius had kept it closed off from the collective and told the others the importance of family benefited us all.

"I know this, so what is your point?" Only a handful of

our kind knew what the end of Nyx would mean for this realm—the end.

Casimir scrutinized Drew. "This is Albert's boy?"

I glared at her hateful face, ready to push between her and him if she made a move.

Leana shifted to a protective stance. "He is the brother of Gemma and Arianna and has a destiny of his own."

"Why can I not see his magic?" she asked, annoyance in her tone.

Ahh...I'd forgotten she could read both fae and unicorn magic.

"My guess would be because he is part sprite." I took way more pleasure in sharing that news than I should have.

She jerked her head toward me. "That's impossible."

"Is it?" I smirked, loving that I knew something before the smug know-it-all. She usually did have the answers, so this was a rare moment. "The sprites we met on the sacred mountain believed it to be true."

"No one can traverse the mountain."

"It was not without difficulty," Leana said, her voice low.

No, it was hard as fuck. I didn't want to share that with Casimir, but I had to deal with her to get to Phina's location. "Drew was called there, and the sprites came to him. They crossed the realms to meet us at the sacred place and explain his destiny."

"Which is?" Casimir asked.

"Something I'll share with our leader first." I refused to give her info to go running to my brother like some savior.

"If the sprites have returned, we need to discuss—"

"They only came for Drew and returned to whatever realm they've been in for centuries." I cut her off. She didn't have the upper hand, and she didn't like it clearly.

She narrowed her eyes at me. "I could have you locked up, Cyrus."

"But you won't because my brother would be disappointed in you. He might even punish you...then again, you might enjoy that."

She scoffed. "Enough of this asinine conversation. Let me show you to the secluded area of the court."

"I need to get to Phina." The quicker I made sure she was okay and she and Drew were safe, the sooner I could get to Gemma and Laurel.

"I'll take you there after we get you and your pregnant match settled."

Leana gasped. "How did you—"

"I can smell it on you," Casimir said, her voice softer. "Others will too."

Interesting. I had caught no whiff of scent from her that differed. Leana looked at me with a similar question on her face. I gave her a single shake of my head. Casimir was gifted, so it was entirely possible she could pick up on a subtle change in chemistry. That meant there were others, as she had said, who might be able to do the same if they got close enough. Leana needed privacy until she was ready to disclose her news.

"How many unicorns are in this secluded space?"

"Not many. Just our representatives here at this fae court."

"You mean spies," Leana said.

"Semantics," Casimir said with a tilt of her head. "But they are here for the survival of this world, so remember that when you start showing and everyone knows you conceived."

Leana positioned herself and Drew on my opposite side from Casimir. *I don't like her.* She sent the message down our bond. I hadn't even realized I'd opened it again, and the message came through so faintly I barely heard it.

I don't either.

Drew covered his mouth and snickered. It hit me that it wasn't Leana's voice in my head. The whisper in my head belonged to Drew. He could communicate like we could. I cut my gaze at Leana to see if she'd heard, but she didn't look as if she had. Casimir kept moving, so I didn't think she'd been privy to the convo either. Could he control who received his messages, like with the unicorn and fae bond?

I wanted to ask Leana if she heard it, but I didn't want to tear down my mental wall for fear Casimir would be in my head and know of Drew's power. Marius trusted her, and that I meant I should. I didn't know how much she shared with the others under her command here, and that stopped me from even entertaining letting her near my thoughts.

"Once I see where you are putting up Leana and Drew, I want to go straight to Phina."

"You act as if you are our leader."

I could pull rank as Marius's proxy, but I wasn't sure that applied here. The fae court had been Casimir's post since before the Great War. No one knew the workings here better than her...not even my brother.

"This way," she said, leading us down a barely worn path in a grove that skirted along the edge of the fae court lands.

Winter wasn't far off. The stronger aroma of decay drifted in the air with the lost foliage of the trees. Winter, indeed, might come early this year, and I could be in the vampire lands when that happened. I'd take all the snow and ice to see Gemma and Laurel healthy and happy.

At least Casimir's first duty was to protect our people. She would do what needed to be done to keep them safe. I worried about what that would mean for Phina and Drew if I left them here with her. Leana would protect them. She personified strength, but as strong as she was, she couldn't stand against Casimir alone. Many feared the old power she embodied. It's probably what made her the right match for Marius. They were equally impressive, but he didn't believe in ruling by fear, and she represented the opposite. She fed on the fear of others, and that worried the fuck out of me—not only for what I would find in the people here but what she might do to Leana for fun.

CHAPTER 15
A CLEAR PASS

Casimir routed us to the far corner of the palace grounds, a secluded but well-maintained area. I'd visited the space when Gemma and I arrived about five years ago. She'd been so curious about the city and the technology and Laurel and couldn't wait to drive a car. I relished the memory. I would let her drive me wherever she wanted once she was safe in the palace again. While the unicorns who resided here seemed quite comfortable, I chose missions to escape the area. It was too modern for me, and it looked like they'd continued to innovate in the time I was gone. If Leana was comfortable and the children safe, then the significance of my feelings mattered not.

"Here are the homes of our people. There are several open ones, and I had one set up for you." The quarters essentially looked like a fancy set of individual barns to me, but Casimir appeared proud. "We don't want to take on too much of the fae architecture."

I nodded. Screw the architecture. I wanted to know if the house was defendable should there be an attack. "Show us where we'll be."

She led us to the one on the far end. "I figured you wouldn't want neighbors next door."

"No, we do not. That was considerate." She didn't want them close, either, was the message.

She glamoured into her faelike form, and I'd never seen her in this manifestation all these years. Casimir appeared as a young blonde woman with very few clothes on. I almost chuckled at how innocent she looked, but I surmised she would drive her horn through my heart if I did. She opened the door.

The outside was misleading. Inside, the home looked modern and had plenty of technology to create comfort, including the television most fae prized. I didn't like those squawk boxes. They made the fae lazy, and they believed too much of what they saw on there. The unicorn shows were atrocious, but the children did seem to enjoy them. I wanted to kick both back hooves into the screen the first time I saw the animated version after Gemma and I arrived here.

"Is it to your standards, Cyrus?" Casimir asked, looking at her nails.

"Yes, this will be fine." I turned to Leana. She appraised the area and didn't seem put off by what she saw. Drew ran a toy car across the wood plank floor. "Why don't you and Drew get settled while I go get Phina?"

"Shouldn't be too hard. Looks like everything is at our fingertips." Leana met my gaze, and worry filled her eyes so heavily I wasn't sure I should leave. "We'll see you soon."

"Soon," I said and followed Casimir out of the dwelling.

Casimir led me through a different, well-worn path toward the palace I'd familiarized myself with during my first time here. The structure stood on two levels above ground and one below with a far more modern facade than the castle where Gemma and Arianna grew up. More fae moved about as we reached a street—many bowing their heads in respect. "I rarely glamour here, but if the attention makes you uncomfortable, feel free to."

"I visited here before, Casimir. They have seen me."

"Oh, yes, it was so brief I'd forgotten."

Normally, I'd welcome trading verbal jabs with her, but I wanted to get to Phina. I gave no fucks about exchanging insults at this point.

"The gate is a couple of blocks ahead."

"Good. I'm anxious to see how Phina is doing and who is taking care of her."

Casimir tsked at me. "Do you really think a princess of this court wouldn't be cared for, especially after the attack Albert launched? You haven't asked about it, and I suspect I know why."

I was worried about my thoughts being open to the collective, but she announced events like they were common knowledge. "Do you always speak so freely in an open street?"

"I have nothing to say to you they don't already know."

My spine went rigid with anger. I let out a sigh and tried to keep my irritation at bay. Seeing two unicorns, especially those close to the leader, brawl in the streets of the fae court wouldn't be a good example. Nor would such actions help with relations as we brought the others to this area.

"Do you want to hear about how the false king struck?"

"If I say no, you're going to tell me anyway."

"He attacked the stadium where the fae were playing Moirai—that stupid game where they run up and down the field with a ball both princes love. Rainier and Laurel underestimated Albert's ability to sneak into the court undetected. He caught them by surprise and spilled a lot of fae blood before he took your precious charge and her mate."

The anger I'd tamped down bubbled up like it would explode. I took several deep breaths, calming the eruption to a dull roar. Casimir led us through the gates of the palace grounds. The guards nodded in her direction and ignored me.

"It's infuriating, isn't it?" she continued. "That he could sneak through not only himself but, also, so many vampires. How could that size of a force get through without tripping an alarm? It's almost as if they had help." She stopped and studied me as if she waited for me to arrive at the same conclusion.

"You think there is a traitor among us?" I must not be who she suspected for her to have shared this much with me.

She tilted her head to her shoulder. "Who's to say? Wouldn't it be awful if it was someone close to us who had given him a clear pass to the court?"

Casimir didn't just think there was a traitor but thought it was someone we both knew. I didn't hide my disbelief that she appeared to be insinuating it was a unicorn. She couldn't mean my brother. He wouldn't ever put Arianna in that kind of danger.

"It wasn't me, and I know you can't mean Marius."

She deadpanned her gaze at me. "I am definitely not referring to you or your brother." She paused. "Or anyone else, for that matter." She shook her mane out. "Come. Phina is this way."

CHAPTER 16

RECOGNITION

Phina played a game on the television with another child. She was the spitting image of Gemma at the same age. I'd missed so much, but as soon as I saw her, I could see her parents, but I believed what the sprite said too. I watched Phina for a minute in silence, letting her enjoy this last moment of peace before we turned her world upside down. Then again, hadn't her world been turned upside down already with her parents being kidnapped?

She stopped playing and raised her head. She found me and recognition crossed her face. My throat thickened. She was my daughter, not by blood but by magic, and I would love her and protect her with my life. Phina hadn't met me. She couldn't know me, so I assumed it must be Casimir she recognized. Her gaze landed on me, though.

Casimir inclined her head toward a woman who had been sitting with the children, and the gray-haired woman led the other child out of the room.

"Cyrus?" Phina stood, and a broad smile crossed her face. She ran across the room. "I knew you would come."

I lowered my head to her, and she wrapped her tiny arms around the bridge of my nose. She hugged me as if she'd known me since birth. *Thank Erebus. She is safe.* I held my horn high, careful not to let it come near the child. Even at this young age, her power radiated around her, and as the sprite said, I could feel our powers mixed. My heart clenched. I glamoured into my human form and dropped to a knee. "Princess Daphina, I'm so happy to meet you."

She climbed onto my knee and wrapped her arms around my neck, giving me one of those giant hugs only a child was capable of doing. "Cyrus, we've known each other my whole life. You are the reason I am here. I knew even before Mommy and Daddy told me the story."

I choked back a sob, biting back my tears. Her mental development seemed so much wiser than her years. "They told you of my gift?"

"Yes, I carry it inside me." Her words were true, and she seemed to understand what that meant. The child reached for the dampness on my cheek and held her small hand out to me.

"You keep it." I closed her fingers loosely to cradle it. "Do you have something to put it in?"

"Of course." Her hand still extended, she opened her tiny fist up. The tear soaked into her skin as if it recognized the part of me in her. "Is that okay?"

"That is more than okay. It is perfect." I hugged her to me. The sprite hadn't been lying. I'd found my family. My throat tightened, and I took a breath to relax it. "I promise to keep you safe just as I would your mother or your father."

"Mommy told me that too. She said you would come one day."

I sniffed, holding back more tears. "Did she?"

"Yes, she knew you would return when it was time, and we would finally be the family we were meant to be. They missed you. I did too."

Erebus, I'd been such an idiot.

"Then we shall be whatever family you want to be." She hugged me tight, and if she'd been older, I might not have been able to breathe. "Maybe I can call you Phina like your mommy and daddy?"

"Why wouldn't you? That's what Mommy, Daddy, Ari, Rain, and Marius all call me. It's my name."

I nodded. "So, it is." I stood, settling her on my hip. The guilt of my choices weighed on me. Had I not left, this talk might not even be necessary. "I need you to be really brave for me."

"Mommy says I'm the bravest. Daddy says I'm stubborn like her."

I chuckled. "Both can be true.

She scrunched up her nose. "I suppose." She sounded so much like Gemma, and I wanted her to grow up with her mother to see that for herself.

"I'm going to take you to meet some new friends. My friend, Leana, and your uncle, Drew. You haven't met him yet, but he's not much older than you, so I think you'll be fast friends."

"Drew has come to my dreams. We've played a bunch."

I didn't want to contradict her, and with what I'd seen from Drew's powers, I believed her. She looked so serious.

"When you meet him, you'll have to let me know that he is the boy you know from your dreams."

"Okay. Are we going now?"

"Yes, but we can gather some of your things first."

Casimir stepped forward. She'd been so quiet I'd forgotten she was there. No doubt she learned more than I cared for her to know about my relationships. "Her room is one floor up. We can go collect her things there."

"Will you carry me, Cyrus?" Phina asked. "I like how our magic hums together."

"Hums?" I asked, glancing between us.

"Listen," she said.

My suspicion was the sound she heard was my magic being drawn to its parts, but I couldn't hear the noise. "I think that whisper might be just for you, Phina, but I will carry you."

CHAPTER 17

THE PAINTING

Phina gathered a doll and some snacks, even though Casimir assured her she could get more, and we weren't going that far. I knelt to her level. "Will you choose a few of your favorite outfits to take too?"

"How many?" she asked me. "I can count to a hundred, you know."

"I don't think you'll need a hundred. How about five?"

"Okay." She skipped off to her room.

I stayed in the living room with Casimir. As soon as she moved out of hearing range, Casimir whirled on me. "The rumors are true. Your magic runs in her."

I sighed, knowing lying to her was pointless. Unicorns would think the impossible had happened if I didn't tell the truth. "It does, but not how you think."

"How did this happen?"

"I didn't even know it was possible. The sprite told me

it had happened with the tear I left Gemma for Phina's birth."

She narrowed her eyes at me. "You swear you didn't know?"

I wasn't sure why it mattered to her if I knew or not. "I swear on my own life, Casimir."

She turned a scrutinizing gaze on me for what felt like an eternity. Then she relaxed as if she'd heard the answer she needed to hear. "I'd like to hear about these sprites."

"I'm sure you would and will...after I tell my brother." She didn't care as much about the mixing of my magic with Phina's as she wanted to catch me off guard to talk about the sprites.

She huffed. "He would be fine with you telling me."

"I have no doubt he would, but he should know first. Besides, you said there is a traitor among us. How do I not know you are the traitor?"

Her mouth curled in a wicked snarl. "If I was the traitor, you wouldn't be standing here, but I do appreciate that your eyes are opened to the possibility now."

I laughed and shook my head. She was something else, and I could almost see what Marius liked about her. Casimir was full of fire, and Marius needed passion around him. He was far too calm.

"Why do you allow him to..." Phina rounded the corner, and I let my question go. She held some clothes in her hand.

"How about we put those in a bag to carry them?" Casimir said, changing into her faelike form. She took Phina's hand and led her back to the room.

I followed them and leaned against the doorframe. Casimir rummaged through the closet. I took in the child's room. The space, rather large for even a high-born fae child, featured fae toys and numerous games and puzzles that required critical thinking, innovation, and problem-solving. Phina was bright, so I figured her parents wanted to make sure she had plenty of science, technology, engineering, and math activities to keep her progressing.

In a painting on the wall, Phina stood in front of her parents. The perfect family portrait hung of them. Beside Gemma was a unicorn. I moved closer to examine. The figure was me. My hands shook, and I crossed my arms over my chest to hide them. Only my location should be in the usual place of a guard—the normal position behind the charge, but I hadn't been situated in the shadows. No, I'd been put in a place of prominence next to Gemma. I stifled a gasp. A tiny purple butterfly, like the ones in my dream on the mountain, hovered beside me. The rest of my body shook like my hands. It was a beautiful family, and I was part of it.

"Isn't it perfect, Cyrus?" Phina planted herself next to me, looking up at the painting.

I smiled and closed my eyes briefly. "It is. Do you know who painted this?"

"It was me," she tilted her chin up and smiled.

I was shocked. The painting looked like something an artist would have done. "You did this by yourself?"

"I did," she said with confidence, but then she deflated a bit. "Is it bad? Mommy said I painted good."

"It's very good, Phina. Many do not know this, but

your grandmother, for whom you are named, painted. Some of her paintings are in the gallery here."

Her face lit up. "I've heard stories about her, but Mommy said I am too young to go to the museum. She promised to take me one day when I am older."

"Your mommy is smart. You should listen to her on this one. One day will be the right day to visit."

"Will you go with us when she takes me?"

"Of course, if it's okay with both of you when that time comes."

She danced around in a circle.

I held my hand out to her. If we wanted that day to happen, I needed to get to her mommy and daddy sooner rather than later. "We'd better go."

"So, you can rescue Mommy and Daddy?"

I knelt to her level. "Who told you they needed rescuing?"

"I see them sometimes..." She pointed to her head. "In my mind. I've seen them, and they don't look good."

My stomach bottomed out, followed by a rush of anger. No child should have to see an image like that of her parents. I pushed my anger back before I spoke to her. "I'm sorry you had to see that image of your mommy and daddy, but I will bring them home to you."

"Of course, you will." She hugged me tightly. "You are special."

It meant more hearing it from her than the sprite. She was meant to have a destiny we must all protect, and I connected several of the signs that occurred in our present times. Arianna had more than General Daphina's powers, and we suspected she had everything Nyx had to give her. Gemma, incredibly powerful in her own right, mothered a gifted child whose powers rivaled her aunt's. Drew was part of all of us, and his power grew daily. In my lifetime or my parents' generation, we had never experienced a magical shift like happened at present. Our realm dangled at a turning point, and our lives were never going to be the same.

CHAPTER 18
CHAINS

Phina ran toward Drew, and he toward her. They hugged each other like long-lost friends. Smiles adorned each of their faces. I took their embrace in the doorway as a good sign. Leana's mouth opened, but nothing came out.

I let my wall down. *Apparently, they have been playing together in their dreams.*

Seriously? Since when do fae have such power?

Fae do not.

His sprite side.

Yes, he visited her. Somehow, he knew they were meant to help each other, I suppose.

Bring Phina's parents home.

Leana turned to the children. "Come inside. Let's get Phina settled."

They followed her in and I did, too, to tell the children goodbye. It was time for me to do my duty, and the urgency to leave had ramped up in my blood now that I knew Phina was safe.

Leana walked me outside the home, and Casimir followed. Casimir stepped closer. I saw a slight tremor in her mane, but it disappeared as quickly as I saw it.

"Marius asked me to stay here and defend the fae court no matter what happens. Should any threat come for the children, I will make sure Leana has as much time as possible to get them to safety." With no pretense in her tone, it was the nicest thing she'd said since I'd known her. I appreciated her effort.

"Thank you." I nodded to her. She gave one swift nod in return.

"Don't do anything stupid, Cyrus. I know how you and Marius are when you are together," Leana said. "You need to make good choices and come home. Drew doesn't need any more heartbreak."

"Neither does Phina," I said. "They've both seen more than those their age should have seen in a lifetime. I've taken more time than I should have. I need to go."

"I know," Leana said. "We'll be here when you get back."

"Be smart," Casimir said. "And be careful who you trust."

I gave them both one last look and then ran my fastest for the vampire border.

Marius, I'm headed your way.

Good. We could use you.

Any word on Gemma?

They are still in there, and the vampires must know we found a weakness because their forces have doubled.

Fuck.

Yeah. Fuck is right. Hurry, Brother.

I'm at top speed.

Then shut up and run faster.

I understood what he meant. Time was running out, and I found the strength deep inside me to run even faster.

A blur came toward me. I dodged in the opposite direction. It nailed my hindquarters. I tumbled like one of the boulders down the sacred mountain and crashed into a tree. Stars and black spots dotted my vision. Ringing clouded my hearing, and no other sounds made it in. My body ached as everything went pitch black.

I couldn't open my eyes. No, my eyes were open but covered with a blindfold. *Where the fuck am I?* I tested my legs and met sheer agony as I strained the wounded back leg. The others wouldn't move. They were bound tight. I'd been hit, but by what? And that injured leg? Erebus, it fucking hurt. *Why isn't it healing?*

A sharp pierce invaded my neck. It took everything I had not to cry out or flinch. My senses began to return. I'd been chained to a cold stone slab. My lifeforce fought against the feeling at my neck. My blood was being drained away by some device. War made this seem like child's play, but this was bad—I was a prisoner.

Vampires? No, I'd be dead. They wouldn't have this kind of patience. What then? We had no other predators. Who would be so stupid?

I reached down my twin bond to my brother. *Marius? I'm trapped.*

No response. I didn't panic. I'd been cornered and trapped many times in battle. The others could already be clashing with the vampires. I was going to have to figure my own way out of the situation.

Marius? Can you hear me? I've been captured and am injured.

I waited for what seemed like an eternity. In reality, only a few minutes passed, but it was long enough. My messages weren't getting through. Either I'd become too weak from the injury and blood loss, or something here dampened the ability to connect. This was worse than I thought. The cell was built for not only the containment of an individual but also their magic.

A rustling sound permeated the silence. The piercing at my neck eased, and the needle slid out. It hit me. The goal wasn't to kill me or drain me. My captor intended to use me for my blood—unicorn blood. I had to free myself and fight, but my injured leg hadn't healed, which meant the wound might be severe. They would not drain me dry. *Fuck it. It doesn't matter. I'm fighting my way out and taking this fucker down with me if I go.*

I slowed my breathing to imitate sleep. A hand brushed over where my blood had been drawn from. I fought the urge to flinch from the contact. The touch stopped, and footsteps drifted away. I waited a few minutes in case the being had hearing like ours. I couldn't sense their kind, so they'd found a way to block my powers in the cell at the very least.

Glamouring was lower vibration magic and might be dampened, but not completely blocked. If I glamoured to my faelike form, it would be easy to slip out of the bonds, but my injured leg might not heal right if I did. I could always have it rebroken to heal properly, but I had no idea what I faced outside of this room. I might need all my power, including physical, to get free. *How did I not sense the pending attack? Godsdammit.*

I focused on my injured leg and sent healing energy there. The tendons, bone, and muscle all protested, but the angry protest gave way to painful healing. A sweat broke out along my brow, and I bit down on my lip. It took more out of me than it should, and I only got about halfway before I had to stop. Exhaustion claimed me from the action. My lids weighed a thousand pounds, and I could no longer keep them open. A purple butterfly drifted through my mind as sleep overtook me.

I woke, very aware that another being inhabited the room with me. Was it a sprite? My mind drew a blank on who else could pull this off other than multiple vampires or sprites. I kept my breathing in a steady state to simulate sleep. I needed to learn as much as I could, and I'd stand a better chance if the captor believed me to be unconscious.

A gentle hand stroked the hair from behind my ear down to my shoulder, almost as if it cared about the pain it inflicted on me. Care or not, this was wrong, and I'd have my revenge. A jab stung my neck, and I managed to avoid flinching for the second time. Blood drained from me once again. There was much that could be done with my blood, so this was probably a rogue fae looking to sell under the market. I doubted I'd become the first victim, and I wanted nothing more than at the first opportunity to shove my horn through the perpetrator.

As last time, the being removed the needle and left me alone. My strength hadn't fully returned. I grew weaker, but I had to get that leg healed before I could get out of the cell. I sent every ounce of magic, lessened in strength but still there, I could muster toward it. The wound responded faster, and the healing went further this time. I was close... close enough to get the fuck out of here.

I glamoured into my fae-ish form and slipped out of the chains. They were heavy—much heavier than they should have been. Everything in this room had been designed to keep my powers at bay, and the drain suffocated me. I ripped the blindfold away and saw walls made of a stone I hadn't seen since the war. It'd been banned in the kingdom, and there was only one place I knew that still used it—the vampire lands. But if I'd been brought that kind of distance, the being had delivered me closer to my goal. My heart constricted, twisting in a painful distraction from my leg. *Gemma. Laurel. I will find you.*

CHAPTER 19

THE CELL

How long had I been out? Vampires were fast, but they didn't move as fast as we did. Could they possibly have dragged me that far? They were strong, not as strong as unicorns, but if my captor consisted of more than one, they might be able to do it. If I were in the vampire lands, that distance required me to be out for, at minimum, hours for them to transport me across the border, and probably days, depending on how deep they took me into the vampire kingdom.

I inhaled the tainted scent of the room for any changes since I'd been out. Rotten metal and death hit me like the sting of a cold winter morning. Fae, unicorn, and animals—they'd all died in this room or nearby. I was fucked big time. I ran my hand along the cool, obsidian-colored stone. The drain was painful on my power. I jerked my hand away. The dark glint might look like the precious stone, but it wasn't. I'd known, but I needed the physical confirmation. I was never going to get to full strength in this room. I could see well enough without light in here, but the door was visible. Either the entrance had been hidden, or it could only be opened from outside. This room had been designed for one thing, and that wasn't escape. I'd faced four dozen vampires on my own in battles—probably more if I'd tallied up kills. I didn't know fear then. That version of me existed before Gemma. Since she came into my life, I'd feared for her many times, never myself, always her, but in this room, I feared I might not see her again. Escaping was not going to be a small feat, but I'd keep trying for Gemma and Laurel.

At least in my faelike form on two feet, less of me came in contact with the stone. That would slow the drain and allow some of my power to replenish. My injured leg throbbed, but I wouldn't sit down. Not when it meant losing any little bit of force I could build inside me.

I slowed my breathing and focused on manifesting calm as I opened my mind to Gemma. I had to know she was still fighting. My mind timidly pushed down the bond to ease against her end. I didn't want to panic her. She had enough to worry about. I wanted her to know Phina made it to safety with Leana. That had been my plan to contact her after I spoke to Marius. I readied myself for it to be blocked by the unicorn collective, but a unicorn and charge's connection behaved differently—bound by magic from Nyx and Erebus themselves. *Erebus, let this work.*

Like a gentle breeze, I blew into her mind. *Gemma?*

Cyrus? she called back in a groggy voice. Relief washed over me, and my demeanor required deeper focus. I had no idea what time it was, but I doubted it mattered where Albert had her and Laurel. If he'd hurt her more...

Did they touch you again?

No, I think they are letting me get my strength back so my father can hook me up to his syphoning machine. He's completely crazed. Did you make it to Phina? Drew?

I did. Your daughter, along with your brother, is safely hidden under the protection of Leana.

A heavy sigh drifted from her. *Thank you. And where are you? Are you safe with them?*

I steadied myself. *No, I'm coming to you.*

The guards were talking earlier. I guess they thought I was out. They are worried that my sister and Marius are leading a group in for an attack. I can hear how fearful they are of your brother.

As they should be, he is fierce. He waits for me. I don't think they'll attack before I get there unless something changes.

I'm scared. You probably already sensed it. I'm so afraid for our loved ones trying to rescue us. I'm afraid for you to come here. Part of me wants to tell you to leave me here.

That will never happen. As long as I breathe, I will fight for you—for you both.

Cyrus, I'm worried about Laurel. He's not healing very fast. I'm concerned he's channeling his power to heal me, to the detriment of himself. How do I stop it?

You cannot stop magic shared freely to heal. None of us can, and he is your mate. Sacrifice is part of that Nyx-blessed bond. You can try to channel some of your own.

I'm not sure wind would do any good in this situation.

You have other elements at your fingertips. What about

earth? It is the ultimate rebirth. If you send a small amount of that lifeforce to him, it might keep him from going too far.

Thank you. When the three of us are free, we're going to do things we didn't get the chance to do before. You will know how much we love you.

A twinge of sadness slipped through my wall and down the bond. I tried to pull it back, but it was too late. *That sounds wonderful, Gemma.*

These aren't hollow words.

I know. A noise on the other side of the wall in my cell drew my attention. *I must go. I love you, Gemma.*

*I love—*I slammed the connection closed and shifted into my unicorn form.

The fucker would get me full force and know the wrath of a unicorn who survived the Great War.

The door opened, and a small vampire entered the room. He couldn't have been much past childhood before he'd been turned. I'd guess seventeen or so. His curly brown locks dusted his brow, almost hiding his red eyes, but they glowed in the darkness.

"You are awake," he said, rubbing his hands together. "Excellent."

"Why am I here, vampire?" I pawed the ground.

"We knew you would come this way, and we didn't know how else to get your attention." A female vampire who looked to be about the same age at turning stood next to him.

"There are many easier ways to ask for an audience with a unicorn."

"We need your help."

"I believe you have already helped yourselves," I said, remembering the stings in my neck.

"That wasn't for us." His eyes widened. "We don't require much blood."

I scrutinized him. If they were the oldest of the old, that might be true, but the two didn't have the air of a vampire who had existed for a thousand years.

"It's our mother," the female said. "I'm Jenna, and this is my brother, Kyle. Our mother turned us, but now she's sick. It's like she can't get enough blood."

I'd heard of such a sickness. Some called it the vampire guilt sickness, but others said turning those you loved came at a cost. Whatever it was, it wasn't good. I looked around the chamber. "Why did you put me here?"

"The man who turned my mother owned these lands. He brought his victims here, including our mother. We wanted to make sure we could speak with you, and this room offered a guarantee of that." Kyle said.

"Hmm." Getting out of this room was my top priority, but the similarity of Jenna's name to Gemma chipped at my resolve. "Take me to your mother. I'll see what assistance I can offer."

Jenna clapped her hands together. "Thank you."

Jenna led the way up the stairs.

"I must warn you that she doesn't communicate much," Kyle said. "Her decline is quite hard to witness sometimes."

"I've lived over three hundred years and been through many battles. There isn't much that shocks me."

"She's very sensitive to any light, so we don't even burn candles in her room," Jenna said over her shoulder.

"How long has she been like this?" I asked.

"Shortly after she turned us, she started to decline," Kyle said, regret in his tone. "We just wanted to be like her. She didn't want to make us this way. We kept any food sources away until her hunger became great enough to do it."

"You are both lucky she didn't kill you," I said. "A newly changed vampire has little control."

"Do you think that's what did it?" Jenna asked. "Because she didn't take our lives?"

Vampire disease wasn't a subject I had a lot of knowledge on since we didn't share any sicknesses with them. "I do not know, but take solace in that she loved you enough to spare you."

"She's in here." Jenna pushed the door open. There were no windows in the room, and the stench overpowered my senses. The odor smothered the air like death and rot and decay. I held my breath.

Their mother lay on a filthy mattress, tied to the bed, and weak by vampire standards. The ropes used to hold her in place shouldn't be able to restrain a vampire at all.

"What is her name?"

"Aleria," Kyle said.

"You two stay here. Let me approach on my own."

"She might be calmer with us near," Jenna said.

"No, let me have a moment," I reassured her.

I approached the bed, and Aleria hissed at me like a feral cat. Her eyes were wild like an animal in a trap. I took pity on the weakened predator, backed into a space she didn't feel safe, but I saw no humanity in her. I sensed no spark of memory for life or her children. She snapped at me when I placed my hand on her forehead. *Nyx, grant her peace.*

Aleria was emaciated, and they had taken enough of my blood that she should have been well fed. "Did she normally consume blood after she became vampire?"

I wondered if she wasn't meant to withstand the transformation, but she had succeeded in the process with her children. Both had survived the vulnerable state of a newly created vampire. If she'd tried to change them when she was in the early days of her transformation, she'd likely have killed them. Aleria must have been through that stage to have enough control, and the proof she succeeded stood in front of me.

"Yes, until she changed us. That's when everything deteriorated for her," Kyle said.

"Let's give her space to rest for now. I have a few questions to ask of you."

"We can go to the top floor. It is after dark."

I gestured in front of us. "Lead the way."

The children sat on the grand sofa of a living room where all the furnishings were covered in what appeared to be months of dust. The adornments depicted a home of status and wealth, but the fabrics were threadbare. I wondered again how long they had been turned. Even though they looked like children, their actions seemed older. Any childlike behavior appeared to be more like muscle memory from their old life.

"You say she seemed fine until she changed you?" I asked from where I stood close to the door, ready to flee at a moment should the situation break down.

"Yes," Kyle said. "She made us both in the same night."

I considered the lore I'd heard on vampires and what I'd observed during the Great War. Blood spilled during the war drove some to a madness where they were lost to the consumption of the red liquid. That didn't seem to be the case. Could an anomaly in someone's blood do it?

"This might sound like an odd request, but do you mind if I sniff you or, rather, the vein at your wrist?"

"No, but what will that tell you?"

"It might tell me nothing, or I might find something to explain why your mother is...in an anemic state."

Kyle stood and pulled his sleeve up. I hovered my muzzle a short distance from his vein and inhaled deeply. The vampire blood hit like stagnant water, but there, mixed in with the pungent scent, subsisted the aroma I anticipated.

"Me next?" Jenna asked, holding her wrist out for me.

I inhaled and found the same scent. Telling them felt wrong. Their mother was already lost. While I wanted to be honest, I didn't want to cause them pain, even if they were vampires.

"You know what it is. Don't you?" Kyle pulled his sleeve back down.

"Did you have lots of bruises and nosebleeds when you were human?"

"We did," Jenna said with surprise. "How did you know?"

"Your mother has healed you of that, but you still carry the marker in your veins," I said, treading as lightly as I could but still answering them. Regardless of what I told the siblings, their mother was never going to recover from her current state, and I didn't want an altercation.

"Is that what made her the way she is? Our blood?" Kyle asked.

"I don't know." It was the truth. I didn't understand the

vampire anatomy enough to be sure. I suspected that what healed them decimated her vampire body and ate the last of her humanity away. These children didn't need that burden.

"She's not going to get better?" Jenna asked, her voice quavering.

"I can't say for sure, but I don't believe so," I said. They would likely not face their mother's fate, but I wasn't a healer and had no way of knowing for sure.

"Can you end her suffering? We've discussed it, but we couldn't do it." Kyle's tone was resigned.

Erebus, I wasn't prepared for that question. I'd never been the one to ask for mercy, but I wasn't the unicorn I'd been on the battlefield either.

"Are you sure a step this final is what you want? That is something that cannot be undone."

Jenna looked at Kyle and nodded. He put his arm around her and turned back to me. "We are sure."

"Very well. Do you want to say goodbye to her?"

"Yes." Kyle led Jenna back the way we'd come.

I followed them, remaining silent to let them collect their thoughts.

Kyle paused with his hand on the doorknob. "How will you do it?"

"The quickest way would be with my horn, but there will not be anything left to bury. If it is your wish to have a ceremony and return her to the earth, I can do it in a way that preserves the body."

"That way," Jenna said. "Where we can put her in a resting place we can visit to talk to her."

"Then, I will do as you wish but know you can talk to her from anywhere."

Jenna swiped at her face. Kyle opened the door.

Glamouring into my alternative form, I stood in the hall and listened to the sweet things they said to her, but what nearly broke me was when they told her she would be better soon. Aleria's only response was with hisses and snaps. I didn't blame her. She'd done what she thought would save them. But then the situation left me with a dilemma to either leave them here, wherever the fuck that was, or end them as I normally would vampires. I wondered what kind of blood they consumed if they didn't need much. I assumed their lack of hunger was a side effect of their former life too.

The door opened. Kyle led a tearful Jenna from the room. Red streaks stained their faces. Kyle turned his red eyes up to me. "She's ready."

"And you're sure?" I asked one more time, giving them a chance to stop before there was no turning back.

"No, it's time. She suffers and shouldn't."

I nodded and entered the room. "Hello, Aleria. I'm going to make all the pain go away. I will release you."

Her body stilled as if she understood her children's goodbye or my intention or both. I pulled a chair next to the bed and took one of her bound, withered hands in mine. She didn't react. "Nyx, she was once your child. Erebus, I am yours. May you both have mercy on her and allow her to pass to the afterlife to live out the rest of her days."

I inhaled a breath and regretted it. The rotted stench of the room gagged me. I closed off the air.

Aleria gasped, her gaze trained on the ceiling. I looked up but saw nothing. Her grip tightened on my hand, but I used the other to roll her head to the side, giving me access to the base of the brain. I summoned enough of my power to concentrate it into a stream.

"It will be quick, but you will know what is happening. For the latter, I am sorry, Aleria. I hope you have peace and see your children again someday, far in the future." She hadn't been lucid, but her eyes opened.

"Do it." Her words were a hissing sound, but I could understand them.

Relief that she wanted the end gave me the strength to finish the task. I released her hand from mine to hold her on her side. Her flesh had begun to peel away from her bones. Aleria existed in a constant state of torture. I positioned my finger close and willed the jolt of pure power into her brain stem. The force crackled and sizzled. Aleria's body went slack, and the aroma of burnt death filled the air. No one deserved this. I laid her down and unbound her hands, placing them across her chest. Her eyes gaped open. They were vacant, but I could see peace in them. I swiped my hand over them to close the lids. "Nyx, she is yours once again." At least, I hoped she returned to the goddess.

I gave her one last look and opened the door. "It is done. You may have the burial ceremony whenever you wish."

"We have nothing to repay you for what you have

done," Kyle said, his voice a little quieter than before with a hint of sadness.

"There is no need. All I need to know is where we are, and I will be on my journey." Gemma needed me. I'd done what I could for the vampires—what I think she would have wanted me to do too. But I had to get out of here.

"Can we go with you?" Jenna asked, fear shaking her voice.

They could only travel by night, and that would slow me down. "I'm sorry, but I must make haste in my travels. Others are depending on me."

"Will you come back?" she asked. Red pooled in her eyes.

No part of me wanted to come back, save the pity I felt for them. "Yes, I'll check on you when I return through the area."

"There's a map on the wall in the study," Kyle said. "I can show you where we are on it."

"That would be helpful, yes."

He led us back upstairs to the study angled just off the living room we'd been in before. "Dawn is near. We must hurry."

"Show me where we are, and I can do the rest. You two go where you usually spend the day."

He opened the door, and the room had a layer of dust on it. Kyle pointed to the wall that had a map of the kingdom and the bordering lands.

"Whose house did this belong to?"

"A nobleman named William. We were never allowed to leave here before Mother killed him."

I suspected they were his children, but the absence of photographs made it impossible to know for sure.

Kyle pointed to a spot on the map. "We're here."

His finger showed they hadn't moved me far at all from my original point of capture—maybe twenty miles at best. I'd be back on track within the hour. "And how long have I been here?"

"Less than a full day," Jenna said. Her gaze darted toward her brother. "We are sorry for how we brought you here. We didn't know another way."

"Everything is meant to be. There are no hard feelings from me." The sunrise peeked through the window and cast a soft glow on the floor. "You better get to your daytime shelter."

Kyle held out his hand. Remaining in my faelike form, I shook it. "Be safe and don't venture far from here. It's not safe for your kind."

"We don't. It's scary out there." Jenna held her arms open for a hug. They were predators, but I suspected the fear from their previous life carried over to this one. Embracing a vampire was dangerous, but a nudge urged me to do it anyway. She held me tight like Phina had when she saw me for the first time.

I pulled back and held her at arm's length. "It will not always be so scary, but you still need to be mindful."

"Until next time," Jenna said.

Kyle nodded.

I returned the gesture. "Until our paths meet again."

CHAPTER 21

IN THE SUN

My leg ached from the repetitive pounding of the pace I maintained. After several hours, I stopped at a stream and waded out until the water covered my hindquarters. The coolness soothed the pain, but it provided the healing properties of the water I craved. In my urgency to get to Gemma, I'd pushed through the pain instead of finding a place I could connect to heal, but that had been a mistake. Traveling the distance left would be impossible in the shape I was in.

I opened my power to the element of water and earth for the rich sediment below my hooves and willed it to my injured leg. Light flitted and swelled in the water and responded in an instant. I sighed at the relief. For the first time since I woke in the dark chamber, the pain in my leg disappeared. The force energized me as if I could run like the wind itself across the countryside. I gave a good shake to free the water from my coat and tested the leg on solid ground. I kicked, jumped, and reared up on my hind legs without any pain. My extremities answered like I'd dialed time back to before the war, when my body hadn't sustained hundreds of injuries.

The sweet grass aroma of the glen ahead drifted around me, and I took off in an easy run. No pain. I stepped up the pace to a moderate run. Nothing. I opened to full speed, and the landscape blurred around me. I kept my senses on alert as I maintained the same pace I was in when the children were able to reach me. I'd been complacent—something I'd never done before and would not allow myself to do again. While the daylight hours were less vulnerable, I perpetually scanned my surroundings.

I crossed into the forest that made up the outer lands of the fae kingdom. The woodlands on this side had never seen battle in the Great War, so no spirits were trapped here. The lush vegetation teemed with life of all kinds. On a different day, I might have stopped to listen to the melody of the birds or watch for the black deer that were said to be touched by Erebus. Others believed them to be personal creations of Nyx's consort and linked to his magic. The last time I saw one was before the Great War while out exploring with my brother. Marius had shifted to his faelike form, and I followed. It was the first time I realized how long I could hold my alternate persona. My brother and I crouched as small as we could and watched the deer come so close to us we could touch it. Neither of us moved, but the deer had stretched its neck out toward me. The animal's eyes, solid black, settled on mine. Then, it turned and ran so fast I wasn't sure we could have caught it if we tried. I sighed, letting the memory fade away with my breath.

The sun dropped low in the sky, and darkness would soon be upon me. Another day where I hadn't looked up the two fae I loved. Eventually, on the other side of the forest, I'd emerge at the border of the vampire lands. I slowed my pace. The chances of meeting a vampire, even a rogue one, increased here. There were many, both fae and unicorn, claimed here whether they were on patrol or not. This area was vulnerable for all of us, so every snap of a twig or breeze deserved scrutiny.

I'm in the forest. I should be there in a matter of hours. The message skated down the twin bond to my brother.

Can you home in on my location? he responded.

I couldn't determine with precision—only that I was headed in the right direction. *Not yet, but I should soon.*

Good. You are close. We'll wait for you before we make our next move.

I'm ready to get my...charge. I caught myself before I said woman, but the word that flitted on my tongue was mate. That couldn't be, though. A unicorn could not be mated to their charge, and the honor of Gemma's mate belonged to Laurel. It must have been a slip in my mind, thinking of their safety.

Stay vigilant. The woods are not safe.

Noted. I cut the communication off because my mind played "mate" on repeat in my thoughts. I didn't want to chance Marius hearing that word and drawing his own conclusions before I even understood why it haunted me.

The odor of decay hit me fast. I jerked my head in the

direction from which the wind blew. If it was a vampire, I needed to handle the situation and not allow the predator to follow me to the others. It might be a rogue encounter, but more than likely, it would be a scout for our enemy.

I glamoured into my faelike form so I could conceal myself more easily behind the trees. My steps were light like the fae when they used their earth element magic. The scent grew stronger and indicated more than one. I'd shift into my natural form and destroy them when I found them—quick and efficient.

Whispers drifted on the wind. "I think he went this way. I smell him."

I let my glamour go and stepped into their path, ready to attack, but leaving enough distance to be out of reach. Shock shattered my composure. Kyle and Jenna stood before me. "How are you here?"

Their mouths gaped open and their eyes widened in eerie unison. "We followed you."

"In the sun?" I asked, confused about how they weren't turning to ash, especially since they'd been concerned about dawn's approach.

"We thought only the nobleman and Mother were the ones who couldn't walk in the sun after she turned. Then, Mother brought others who couldn't, and we realized we were different. We always have been able to take the light."

My shock doubled. "How?"

They exchanged a look, and Jenna shrugged. "We just do, but we've always hidden it out of fear of the others who couldn't."

I sensed their unease. It wasn't of the sun but of what other vampires might use them for to see if they could walk in the sun too. "And you don't consume a tonic or herb that allows you to do so?" The vampire reserved those special treatments for their soldiers, and unicorn or fae blood served as the base for most of those concoctions.

Kyle scrunched up his face. "No."

"You shouldn't have come here." Their isolated lands offered some protection, but there was none here if they were caught. The vampires might not even spare them, especially given Albert's penchant for test subjects. "You have put us both in danger."

Jenna's lip trembled. "We didn't want to be alone. With Mother gone and you leaving, we didn't have anyone else."

They were too young to be turned—unable to exist on their own. The children were technically the enemy. I should have destroyed them when I first saw them, but I couldn't make myself do it then any more than I could now.

"Go back to your home. I promise to visit when I am there again." I softened my tone.

"We lived there, but it was never our home," Jenna said.

I stared up into the tree canopy as if the answer would fall like a leaf from one of the trees. "You cannot come with me."

"Why?" Kyle asked.

His question would have been fair any other time, but

I'd risk more than my own life telling them the truth. "Because I said so."

"Where do we go?" Jenna asked.

"To live with others of your kind who can teach you how to survive."

Kyle shook his head. "They know we are different, even if we conceal it from them. Mother tried to introduce us to a couple before she was...completely lost."

"And where is the couple now?"

"She had to end them," Kyle said, matter-of-factly. "They threatened to tell others about us, and Mother thought..."

"They would kill you," I finished for him. Marius would think I'd lost my mind if I showed up with two turned vampire children. I couldn't leave them in the woods or worse, have them follow me farther only for our guards to end them. "You must do exactly as I say and stay close to me. If I tell you to hide, you do so without question. If I tell you to run, you move as far away as you can at top speed. Are we clear?"

Jenna smiled. "Yes."

It hadn't escaped me that I seemed to be collecting children—fae, a child that consisted of all of us, and now these vampire children. And here I thought I'd never be a parent, and I was by far the least equipped unicorn to be one. "Let's get moving."

When I felt Marius's location becoming clearer, I stopped to reach out and explain my guests and braced for his response. *Brother, I know your location.*

Good. We're finalizing our plans based on the latest recon.

I need to tell you something.

Are you okay?

I have two children with me.

This is no place for fae children.

They are not fae.

Concern permeated the line between us. *What do you mean?*

They are two vampire children, and before you call on Erebus to take me, they are not like other vampires.

Cyrus. Marius sighed. *The vampires often use children as spies.*

I looked at Jenna and Kyle. *They are not spies, but I think we could learn much from them.*

Marius let out a longer, louder breath. *Fine, but they are your responsibility. I will not give up anyone to babysit them. If they harm any of us or betray us, it is on you.*

I agree to these terms.

Get your ass here.

Be there shortly.

"We are close to meeting the others I came for. I need you to keep your heads down and hands to yourself. There might be some temptation you will encounter but tell me if you do. We'll go hunt for animals."

"Are you going to protect us?" Jenna's eyes widened.

"As much as I can, but you have to understand you will be around many who will not trust you no matter what you do." I wasn't sure I trusted them, but I wouldn't turn my back on them either. *Erebus, I hope I'm doing the right thing.*

"We won't cause any trouble," Kyle said. "We'll do whatever you say as long as we're not alone."

CHAPTER 22

DEATH NEVER LEAVES

The scowls were on me not the children, so I figured Marius told the others to not fuck with me or my guests. The sky dimmed to a pale cast of color, but the obvious detail that my companions had traveled during the day to arrive at dusk seemed to escape no one. A target would be on their backs because vampires couldn't do that without help in the form of fae or unicorn blood.

I followed the twin bond to the center of the camp until my brother, with his black coat and white mane, came into view. The twin bond hummed with my arrival, sending my happiness to him. His head raised, and he took quick strides toward me. He glamoured into his faelike form with a smile on his face, and I did the same. While we were opposites in our natural forms, we looked much more similar in our faelike embodiment—not mirror reflections or copies, but closer. Marius's eyes were more black and mine more blue, and his hair was ink-black where mine had streaks of gray. He stood a couple of inches taller than me and never failed to remind me of that when we were younger. My twin gathered me in a warm embrace, and not like I'd disappeared and resurfaced with two vampire children.

"I've missed you, Brother," he said, joy in his voice.

"And I you." I held onto him for an extra moment, thankful to lay eyes on my twin.

"Introduce me to your friends," he said, shifting back to his majestic form.

I remained in my alternate persona. "Meet Kyle and Jenna."

The children looked stunned and were vampire-still. Jenna's mouth slid open, but nothing came out. I inched closer in hopes that would give them some sense of safety.

"My name is Marius. I lead the unicorns, and my brother, Cyrus, is who brought you here." Standing twenty-two hands high and taller than my own twenty, he towered over the children.

Slowly, their expressions morphed into fear. The children looked so terrified, I thought they might burst into flames. Neither uttered a syllable. Whispers filtered through the camp as if carried by the wind. Vampires couldn't walk in the day without some major assistance, and these children didn't have the means for that help.

Marius observed them in careful consideration, and I could feel his inhale. "You are vampire but not."

Kyle and Jenna looked at me as if they expected me to speak for them, and I didn't know what to say on their behalf. I surveyed the others watching, and far too many curious and hateful stares peered our way. "Perhaps there is somewhere we could go talk where not as many eyes are upon us."

Marius glanced up and gazes from across the camp averted. "My tent."

My brother led us to the large structure standing next to one of equal size, but both stood a distance from the others. Arianna and Rainier stood outside the other one. Her forehead was bunched up, and my stomach clenched, thinking she might have heard something about Gemma. Rainier rubbed her upper arms, and she relaxed. I blew out a breath and prepared for her scorn. She commanded fire with ease, and I imagined myself dodging her fireballs. An image of the little girl who had wrapped herself around my leg because she thought I was taking her sister away came to my mind. She didn't like Gemma disappearing to train with me. I'd heard what Arianna's father had done to her, yet she remained steadfast for her sister. Her strength and bravery were a gift from Nyx.

I inclined my head toward her. "Arianna." And then did the same to her betrothed. "Rainier."

Arianna's sharp gaze narrowed at me. "She needed you."

Failure filled every fiber of my body. Regret crept in to settle alongside it. I bit down on my lip. "You're right. She did, but I ensured your brother and her daughter were taken to a safe haven. I don't deserve her forgiveness, but she gave it freely anyway. I will secure her safety here."

She threw open the flap of her tent and marched inside.

Rainier paused. "Give Ari some time."

I nodded, recognizing the hurt Arianna dealt with as similar to my own, and followed my brother into his tent. The vampire children stayed close to me.

"He's right. Ari has been through her worst nightmares over the last few months. She'll come around in her own time."

"I made my choices, and I expect forgiveness from no one." If Ari didn't forgive me, I could live with it. Her absolution, while welcome, wasn't needed, but it would make things easier for Gemma.

"Children, please sit." Marius gestured to a table big enough for four. I took a seat with them. My brother switched back to his faelike form and joined us. He looked at me. "How did you meet Kyle and Jenna?"

If I told him they trapped me, he wouldn't trust them, even with me sitting here in front of him. To lie to him would be treason, but I'd save the beginning of the tale for later. "At their mother's estate."

"And where is she now?"

"She is no longer with us," Jenna said, looking up. "We pray she is with Nyx."

I elaborated for my brother to spare the children the pain. "Their mother, Aleria, was afflicted. Some kind of blood sickness. I think it's related to the same illness the children had when they were human."

The blood sickness they had as humans still marked their blood, but the vampirism appeared to have healed its effects. A healer needed to look at them, but they seemed healthy otherwise and, from what I'd observed, without consuming large quantities of blood.

Marius nodded. "I've heard some scattered stories along those lines, and I could smell the difference in their blood from that of other vampires." He looked from Jenna to Kyle. "Is it not hard for you to be around us and the fae in camp? Is it not painful?"

He tested their thirst with his line of questioning, and I'd do the same in his position—should have done it. Reminding a young vampire of their cravings had been known to set them into a feral mode. I braced myself for the kids to snarl and lose control. If they needed to be restrained, I would do it, but I didn't want them hurt in the process. I moved closer.

Jenna shook her head, showing no other reaction. She was unaffected, and that was a relief.

"We don't drink much blood," Kyle said, the answer similar to what he'd told me. "Usually, we have a rabbit here and there, but we don't feed on fae or unicorn blood."

While I appreciated they hadn't dined on my people, it did beg the question of how they knew how to catch a unicorn. I'd been distracted, but it was still not an easy task. Kyla and Jenna made it seem effortless.

"You never have?" Marius asked. "Fed on a unicorn or fae?"

"No, Mother heard a story that we wouldn't become what she had if we drank rabbit blood," Kyle said, his voice calm but confident.

The story wasn't true—a tale centuries old. In fact, animal blood wasn't a great substitute for vampires but more an act of desperation. Fae blood, human blood, and unicorn blood were the most potent for them. The only animals I knew of that gave them a similar boost without having magical blood were the horses—probably another reason the horses gravitated to my kind.

"Interesting." Marius rubbed his chin. "And the blood pumping through our veins doesn't appeal to you."

"No, I'm not hungry," Kyle said.

"Neither am I," Jenna added.

"You are highly unusual in the vampire world. I've never met another who had this kind of control," Marius said. "How long have you been vampire?"

"A year, I believe," Kyle said. "We kind of stopped keeping track when Mother got sick."

"After she turned them, she started to decline," I said, gauging my brother's reaction. He focused on the twins with a curious gaze. The kids appeared unfazed by my brother's scrutiny. I was impressed they didn't cower in his presence again after their first experience with him.

"So, your mother died from the sickness?" Marius asked.

The children looked at me, and my brother twisted in his seat, raising an eyebrow to me.

"They said their goodbyes, and I helped them do what needed to be done." A prickling sensation crawled over my skin at the state of the mother and the mercy I'd delivered. Death never leaves. Every existence I'd taken meant something, and I carried each of them with me. Their mother's ending would haunt me despite giving her peace. *Her skin literally separated from the bone, Marius.*

He tilted his head. *You are protective of them.*

I am.

My brother turned back to Kyle and Jenna. "I'll need to ask you to remain in my tent unless Cyrus and I accompany you. Can you abide by my decision?"

Jenna nodded enthusiastically.

"Yes," Kyle said. "We can help gather firewood and other things if you need our help."

The young vampires offered their help, and I appreciated how Kyle wanted to make himself useful. I'd struggled to find my place after the war and before Gemma became my charge. Time had passed, and those days seemed a lifetime ago.

"Let's see how this goes for now and then we can discuss that." Marius tapped the table with his fingers. "And you'll let us know if you are hungry and need to hunt rabbits?"

Kyle nodded this time. "Of course."

Marius stood. "Cyrus, can you come with me? We need to visit another tent."

Leaving them alone gave me unease, but I had to ignore it for my duty to my brother. My brother threw back the flap of the tent and let it fall closed behind him.

"I'll be back later," I said to the children.

Despite my desire to keep them safe, the sole reason I'd come to the border of the vampire lands was to save Gemma and Laurel. Making our family whole was the priority.

CHAPTER 23
TOMORROW

My brother waited for me to join him outside. I blew out a long breath as Marius crossed the short distance to Arianna's tent. Facing Gemma's sister and her fierce temper wasn't high on my list of things I wanted to do, but I deserved whatever anger she dispensed.

"She doesn't want to see me," I said out loud versus down our bond. It served no point in worrying if she would overhear.

"Well, she'll have to get over that if we're going to save her sister." Marius's tone was firm, his voice raised loud enough it would carry through the thin walls.

I cleared my throat and gazed up at the now dark sky. Starlight twinkled in a beautiful dance, but enjoying it was impossible with Gemma and Laurel trapped in Albert's vampire palace.

Marius looked at me with an amused expression. "Are

you afraid of Ari, Cyrus? You've known her since she was a babe."

"No, I'm not afraid of her. I'm afraid of what she is going to think when she hears the truth. Since when do you call her Ari?"

"Since I thought she would die thinking I'd lied to her."

"We have our secrets," I said.

The flap blew open by wind magic. "We all do. Get in here before I use my magic to hurl you inside."

Rainier laughed at Arianna's claim as if he hoped I'd refuse. I swore under my breath and entered. My brother would normally remind her that our kind doesn't answer to fae, but instead, he smirked. He was enjoying this as much as Rainier.

Arianna looked like a queen seated at the table in her tent. "So, tell me how long you were fucking my sister before you ran off and left her."

Erebus, I am not having this conversation with her, Nyx's descendant or not. Rainier spat his wine out and bent over laughing. Marius snorted next to me.

"I'm not sure this is a topic I'm comfortable hearing," Marius said.

"You are in his head. You've certainly been in mine, unwanted. Plus, there isn't enough alcohol in the kingdom to burn the image of you fu—"

"Enough, Ari," Marius said. "You're angry because of your sister's imprisonment, and I know that's triggering for you. Lashing out at those closest to you isn't helping."

She rested her arm on the back of the chair, looking like she could stab him, and turned her head away.

"There are many things you don't know, and I'm not sure it is my place to tell you without your sister here to tell her side." I wanted to explain everything and nothing at the same time, unsure if anyone in this tent would understand the depth of what I felt for Gemma. Gemma deserved a say in how and when and what was said about us, especially to her sister. Would Gemma even want me to recount the details of our relationship?

Arianna didn't look at me. "You mean how you broke your oath and fucked your charge."

My blood simmered in my veins but cooled quickly because Arianna wasn't wrong. I'd ruined every oath I'd sworn, but I still bent to the honor it commanded. "On that oath, I assure you there are things you have not thought of at play."

"Hmm...then tell me before I call on the power of Nyx to obliterate you."

"Arianna." Marius projected a strong and powerful voice—the one he used as the unicorn leader. "That is enough."

She pushed away from the table and stood next to Rainier. He wrapped an arm around her waist and tucked her against his side. She relaxed into him. He was her safe space, and I remembered seeing Gemma do the same with Laurel. She'd done it with me too. Once my two loves were free, I'd not let them out of my sight, and this argument was pointless—a stupid waste of time. She was Gemma's sister and General Daphina's daughter. I reminded myself that her questions and accusations were coming from a place of love, even when she was acting like she'd rather stab me.

"Did you consider that fate might be at work? Two sisters falling for two brothers, both sides from powerful bloodlines." I kept my tone neutral, but inside I wanted to tell her to fuck off.

"Of course, I have. Are you really blaming the Fates for you fucking and flying?"

"We don't fly."

"You know what I mean." She threw her hands in the air.

"I do, so if you will sit down, I will tell you what I feel comfortable sharing until your sister can fill in the entire story for you."

"I'd rather stand."

"Fine." I took a seat and waited. My side was all I'd give. I refused to speculate on Gemma's feelings. Arianna would have to ask her sister for that when she was home.

Arianna pulled a chair away and sat down. Rainier stood behind her as if he, not Marius, guarded her. My brother, for his part, seemed unbothered.

"I'm sure you could tell the bond between me and Gemma grew in a different direction than yours and Marius's."

Her face scrunched up in disgust. "Yes. Anyone with eyes could see that." She paused. "Did you lure her into this relationship?"

I gasped, my stomach roiling. The thought anyone would think that revolted me. "No, it's not like that at all.

She'd matured well into fae adulthood before those kinds of feelings developed from me to her. The change in our connection started for me after the bonding ceremony, and she'd lived two decades at that point. I'd never been in love before, so I didn't know what was happening. Not even with..."

"Leana." Arianna leaned forward. "What does she think of this?"

The petty part of me wanted to tell her that Leana carried a child by another unicorn, so she'd be just fine, but I didn't. "It was hard for her and for me. She has accepted my apology."

"So, she's fine with you coming here to save my sister?" Arianna arched a brow, and it reminded me of her sister.

"She is, and she is guarding your brother and your niece in my absence."

Arianna let out a hard sigh. "I don't know how I feel about it, but Marius says we need you when we break through to free Gemma." She stood again, leveling her glare on me. "I trust him."

"Why don't you and Rainier go for a walk? I can fill Cyrus in on our plan for tomorrow."

"Tomorrow?" I knew they wanted to move soon and had imagined it would be immediately after I arrived.

"Not soon enough for you, or do you need more time to run away?" Arianna said as she left the tent.

"I'm not running away," I called after her. No way she didn't hear me, but the question was if she cared about what I had to say. "I wonder if they have any idea how much alike they are."

"Ari doesn't think she shares any traits with her sister, so I suspect Gemma believes something similar."

I snort-laughed. "You're probably right. So, what's the plan?"

"You're not going to like it, but it's the only way." Marius moved to the map table in the corner, smaller than those in the castles but adequate for our purposes.

I studied the position of the figures and assessed the placement. Malaise twisted to dread and pooled in my stomach. "I'm used to not liking things at this point. Lay it on me."

CHAPTER 24

POSSIBILITIES

The map marked all the boundaries between realms and kingdoms, and the concentration of forces was clear. Marius pointed to a representation of the vampire defenses. "This is the weakest point."

"So, why are your forces concentrated here?" I asked, pointing to the area that defended an entry point to the castle grounds.

Marius placed both hands on the table. "Because we believe that's the closest entry to where Gemma and Laurel are being held."

An unwell feeling churned in my gut and entangled with my anger. "They are underground. I made brief contact with her. Albert's syphoning machine is ready."

"Then it's good we are breaking her out tomorrow." Marius paused, tension returning to his face. "Underground is where the foresight fae believed them to be as well."

"Have they seen us victorious?"

He shook his head. "No, but the last vision came before your arrival. They have a blind spot around Gemma, and they believe that you might be the reason."

A battle we weren't expected to win was something we'd been used to. Me being a blocker to the vision of the future was new. "How so?"

"Have you been blocking your connection to Gemma?"

"Of course, except when I communicate with her."

"They believe that your power might have merged with hers in a way that blocks all others."

I crossed my arms over my chest. So many things were happening that shouldn't be possible. A unicorn and fae had never merged powers to my knowledge. What else in Erebus's name were the Fates going to throw at us? "I've never heard of such a thing. Have you?"

"No, never, but we are in different times. Didn't you mention sprites returning from another realm?"

"I did. They returned for Drew."

Marius's eyebrows drew together. "Drew...that's unexpected."

"The sprites said he's part sprite."

"That would certainly explain the mystery around where his mother had been born. She claimed she didn't know."

I lowered my voice even though no one else should be near his tent. "There's more. They claim he's part unicorn, part fae, part sprite, and part vampire. Could that even be a possibility?"

"Anything is possible when a sprite is involved, so I couldn't rule it out without testing him."

"He commands their power. I've seen it."

Marius rubbed his chin. "This could put him in danger."

"The very reason I left him in Leana's care. Could this, his birth, and the sprites' reappearance be the answer to our reproduction issues?" Leana's pregnancy certainly added a layer of complexity to the situation too. It wasn't my news to tell, but this was my twin brother. He could read my thoughts if he wanted.

"I don't know that it's an immediate answer, but maybe in time."

"Leana is pregnant. It's not mine, and she's not telling everyone yet." The news would be out at some point, and my brother should know as our leader, so telling him wasn't a betrayal.

His eyes widened. "It's not mine either. That is good news for our kind."

"It is, but I wonder if being so close to the sprite homelands had some influence."

"We'll return there and investigate once we have Gemma and Laurel free and their family is safe."

I nodded. "We are in unprecedented times." I debated telling him what the sprite had said about me, but the word popping into my head every time I thought of Gemma was something I couldn't share with anyone else. I wasn't even sure I should talk to him about it, but I opted to broach the latter with him before I drove myself insane overthinking it. "What do you know of mates?"

"Are you asking why your connection with Gemma didn't break when she met Laurel?" he asked, his tone serious with a hint of disbelief.

I hesitated, worried my brother would think less of me or worse, disown me. He knew of my transgressions, but if I questioned whether I could have more, that might cross a line. Would he be forced to be the leader and not the brother I needed? If it were reversed, I'd give him the support he needed, but that had been my role. His was different. I swallowed my pride. "More so for us. Is it possible for me to have a mate with the pairing bond for Leana in place?"

"I think there's a different question you want to ask."

He was right. Perhaps he'd heard some of my thoughts I couldn't shield." Is it possible that Gemma has two mates? One fae and one unicorn?"

My brother gave me a soft smile. "I don't know the ancient origins of mates—only what we were taught from word-of-mouth. The rarity of a mate bond would suggest to a society that someone could only have one."

A part of me deflated, but I tried to hide it from him. If Gemma could have only one mate, that was Laurel. I'd sensed their bond, and they'd both acknowledged it. "That's what I suspected."

"However, there has been nothing I've read or heard that would confirm there is always only one mate for someone."

I looked up. My hope returned in an instant, cautious for what he might say next but praying to Erebus there was a chance. "So, you think it's possible."

A thoughtful expression settled over my brother's features. "Tell me why you believe you might be a mate for Gemma."

"Besides thinking of her whether I'm awake or asleep or every time the sun rises and sets?" My hope came through in my tone, and it was so obvious I was in love. But could it be something more...

Marius laughed. "Yes, some might consider that an obsession, not a mate."

I chuckled. "True. When I think of her, 'mate' is the first word that comes to my mind. At first, I thought it happened because she'd found her mate with Laurel, but it seems like something else. But can a unicorn be mated to a fae?"

Marius patted my shoulder. "As you said, unprecedented times, Brother. I do believe you are mates. The change in your bond with Gemma wasn't an accident. I believe it was the Fates, and if I had to guess, I'd say that's why you never formed the pairing attachment to Leana even though you cared for her."

His casual acceptance was the approval I needed, and I hoped it was a good sign the news would be well received by the others. "How would I know for sure?"

"How do the fae know? How did she know with Laurel?" My brother watched me as if he looked into my soul for the answer.

I lifted a shoulder. "He knew first. She refused to acknowledge the signs until I told her."

"Isn't that the exact kind of self-sacrifice a mate would make? I think your answer might be in that moment."

My brother's point sank into my thoughts, and the answer solidified as if it materialized in front of me. Gemma was my mate too. *Why would Erebus and Nyx do this?*

CHAPTER 25
FATES

Marius and I had finalized the plans for tomorrow's defensive. I needed some air to come to terms with what the realization meant, but Arianna waited for me as I exited her tent.

"I..." She looked down and back at my gaze. "I didn't mean to eavesdrop, but you were in my tent."

"What did you hear?" Bile rose up my throat. Most of that conversation she should have heard from Gemma, not me.

"Enough to know that you are true to my sister and enough to be thankful you are here." She hurried past me into the shelter.

That was probably the closest I'd get to an apology from her. She never did apologize for burning that guard shack down. I thought she targeted me because I'd been in there with the guards playing cards. She'd been jealous of how hard I trained Gemma and begged Marius to train her. He'd been extremely patient, easing her into the exercises. My brother and I had different styles, but each was what our charges had needed. Thinking of Gemma as a charge felt wrong. Our relationship had changed, and so had the bond between us.

Rainier walked past us with a huge smile on his face and a large slice of chocolate cake on his plate. "Cyrus."

"Is that wise before a battle?" I asked.

"It most definitely is," he said, kicking the flap to the tent open.

Marius exited, looking flustered. He nodded as he headed toward where the other unicorns were gathered. Fae and unicorn stood together laughing and telling stories. A fire roared in the center of the circle and cast orangish glows and shadows across the faces—some I recognized and others I didn't. It reminded me of times before the war. I glanced up and found the slight shimmer of a shield cast to hide the location from prying eyes. Not many had the power to produce a shield of that size for an extended period. Rainier had the power, but shields weren't his expertise that I recalled. Arianna was power-ful, but Marius told me shields were a struggle for her. That could have changed in the years since I left. Gemma's skills included wind shields. A piercing pain stabbed my chest as if it were ripping it in two. I closed my eyes and breathed through the agony. When it eased, I took in the group around the fire, seeing my brother fitting right in and knowing simultaneously I didn't belong with them.

I entered my brother's tent to find the children curled up on two cots. They looked like they were sleeping, their bodies nestled under the fur blankets and with their heads cradled by plush pillows. Jenna lay on her side with her hand tucked close to her chin. Kyle faced her from his cot, his body slightly askew and mouth wide open. They looked alive and childlike. But vampires didn't need sleep. I crept closer and watched their chests rise and fall in a rhythm that suggested sleep. "Children?"

Kyle stretched his arms and dangled his legs over the side of the cot. He rose, extending his arms over his head and yawning. Jenna was out cold and didn't stir.

"You sleep?"

"We do. Are we not supposed to?" Kyle reached for the pitcher next to the bed. He poured himself a glass of water. Vampires didn't need water, but he guzzled it down, similar to how Drew had drunk from the stream.

"No, it's perfectly fine. I've just never known a vampire who did."

"Why are we so different?" Kyle set his empty glass on the tray.

"I think it's your blood, but I don't know." I sat at the small table and gestured for Kyle to join me. "Tomorrow, you will need to stay here while we complete our mission. We could be gone most of the day. Do you want to hunt tonight so you will have food for tomorrow?"

"No, we can eat fae food if that's okay."

I nodded. "I'll have some sent to the tent in the morning for you."

"We could be of help, Cyrus," Kyle said. "If they think we're like them, we could help you get through."

I'd sacrifice myself to save Gemma and Laurel, but I couldn't ask two young lives to do the same. If it came down to who to protect, I wouldn't be able to depend on another unicorn or fae to help them. If I were in a position to choose…"I will not ask this of you," I said, doing my best to keep my frustration caged. "The dangers in these lands are far greater than you are used to."

"It's dangerous for us everywhere because we're not like anyone. We owe you. I know Jenna would agree that we want to do this for you. We want to help however we can."

Jenna rustled in her cot and threw her legs over the side. "You two talk so loud." She stood and stretched. "My brother is right. We'll be able to get close to them. I can sense their presence. It's as if our like calls their like."

"They don't seem to notice us," Kyle said. "It's like we're not important enough for them to see."

I considered their offer. They could go where my kind couldn't, get closer than we could, but it was too risky for them. "I will not put your young lives at risk."

"You forget you are not our parent. This is our choice," Kyle said with strong conviction. "We will be fine. What will they do to us?"

He had a point. They would heal from most injuries, and they weren't vulnerable to the sun, which was an advantage over their kind who were working for Albert.

"It will expose your secret to them," I said. The others would be able to smell the difference in their blood. "They might hunt you after they know, for sport or worse." The worst being that the others would drink their blood for a chance to walk in the light.

"You said there are herbs and tonics. They might believe we use them."

"It could work," I said, thinking of how to minimize the risk. If the vampires assumed they were with them because they believed tonics were used, the twins would be given access we'd have to fight our way into. The infiltration could buy additional time. "I'll talk to my brother. He is the leader. The decision is ultimately his."

"But it's your mate we go to rescue," Jenna said, her tone gentle. "You should make the decision."

"Were you listening to our conversation in the other tent?"

"No," Jenna said, crossing her arms in front of her. "Why?"

"Why did you say 'mate' then?"

She shifted her weight between her feet. Vampires didn't need to do that, so it had to be a nervous tell leftover from her human time. "Isn't that who she is? I feel your connection to her. It's almost palpable."

"You're an empath, Jenna," I said, the surprise raising my voice an octave.

"What's that?" she asked.

"Someone who can sense others' feelings and connections. There are even empaths who can influence how others feel."

"So, I have a gift?" Her eyebrows shot up. "I never had a gift while I was fae."

"Maybe your illness made you too weak for it to manifest without hurting you, or maybe turning vampire changed something inside you that made it possible."

"I prefer to think it's that last part. I'm so much stronger now, and I don't have to be afraid."

"That's a very good way to look at it," I said.

"What about me?" The corners of Kyle's mouth turned down, and his shoulders slumped. "Do I have a gift too?"

"I don't know. Sometimes it takes a while to realize we have one or for it to develop. I reached adulthood before some of my unicorn gifts appeared."

Kyle's expression dropped to a morose gaze on the floor.

"Do not give up. You both have many things in common, so it's likely you will have a gift of your own."

His eyes were dark but hopeful when he looked up. "Do you really think so?"

"I do," I said, and I did believe they would. The children were as different from their kind as I was from mine. It would make sense that they were fated for their own destinies. "Just give it time."

"Cyrus, do they have any desserts here?" Jenna asked. "I haven't had dessert in so long."

"The fae are known for their love of chocolate, and the prince of the fae court had a piece of chocolate cake earlier. Let's go see if there is any left in the tent." I had to stop thinking of and treating them like children...right after I made sure they got the dessert they wanted.

CHAPTER 26
MATES

The children returned to their restful state after consuming the cake in the mess tent. The fae gave them a wide berth, but they didn't stare like they had when we arrived, nor did they look at them like predators. Though it was a relief, my guard was still up. Everyone was on edge, and I'd be a fool to think they accepted vampires, knowing we were facing an army of them tomorrow.

I looked at the map, going over the plans in my head. It was a solid strategy with the children sneaking in ahead of us to unlock the doors. I didn't like using them that way, but I'd been their age when I faced my first battle.

A marker denoted the underground chamber where the fae believed Albert kept Gemma and Laurel locked up. Her father bore the responsibility of two of her prisons now—the home where she grew up and the chamber of horrors where he kept my loves. He would know the wrath of the unicorns as he should have two hundred years ago.

Guilt hollowed out my stomach. I regretted the thought because if he had met his end then, Gemma wouldn't be here. I ran my hand over the mark. As much as I'd hated Albert during the war, I could no longer abhor him because the woman I loved existed because of him. My entire being ached to be near her—to hold her, and I reached down the bond as gently as I could, not wanting to cause her any concern or pain. *Gemma?*

I'm here. She sounded drained to the point of exhaustion.

My breath hung in my lungs, unable to move in or out. *Tomorrow. This all ends tomorrow.*

I've been dreaming of us—all four of us with purple butterflies dancing on the wind. She faded away. *I can't wait to see you. And be free...*

Tears stung my eyes, and I pressed the heel of my palms to my eyes. As if I needed another sign, whatever those butterflies symbolized, they connected us. I must have woken Gemma from sleep, but she could sleep all she wanted once we got her out of there.

Gemma? I waited. No response. She needed her strength, so I let her rest. The twinge in our connection, whether the charge bond or what I suspected to be an even stronger kind of attachment, worried me.

I glanced over the plan again. It had to work. I wouldn't leave her in that wretched place another night. I hated the days it had taken me to get here already, even if the detours were for good reasons guided by the Fates. As much as I wanted to ignore those callings, I wouldn't have been able to. The sheer panic that had increased for fear of what Gemma went through, and Laurel too, provided evidence that my own feelings from our bond had been blocked on some level. By whom, I wasn't sure. There weren't many who could manipulate that bond—the Fates, sprites, and on a very rare occasion, there would be a unicorn or fae born with that kind of power. It could have even been one of the children. I reminded myself to stop thinking of them as such. They were vampires after all.

If we survive the day tomorrow, I'd have to figure out where to place them. I couldn't take them to the fae court. If they even allowed the vampires to reside there, the fae would fear them and either ostracize or hurt them or both, and I wouldn't accept another separation from Gemma and Laurel. Besides, I wanted desperately to be part of a family unit and raise Phina with my mate. Could it be mates? Given Gemma and Laurel were destined, could it be we'd been meant to be mated together...all three of us? A fog lifted from my mind as if it had been clouded for weeks—the three of us were mated. I hadn't realized it or even considered it to be a real possibility. I'd loved Gemma with my entire unicorn existence, but what I hadn't noticed before was that I loved Laurel in the same way. *Fucking Erebus.* I had not one but two mates, and I would rescue them both tomorrow.

The tent flaps parted, and my brother entered looking distracted and slightly disheveled. I assumed he'd been training with his charge. He caught sight of me and cocked his head to the side.

"Why do you look as if you've seen a ghost?" He kept his voice low and peered around the tent.

"I have two mates." My shock gave way to realization, and life made sense for the first time in years. I loved two fae. My heart filled with the promise of a future I longed for...as soon as I'd rescued them.

Marius's forehead bunched in confusion. "You said you didn't feel that way about Leana."

"I don't. My mates are Gemma and Laurel." I expected my brother to shun me for breaking an oath—ruining it in the most forbidden way, but saying the words out loud centered me. The rightness of what I'd declared warmed the center of my chest. I surrendered to the feeling. No matter what anyone else, unicorn or fae, thought, I belonged to Gemma and Laurel and they to me. *My mates. Mine.*

A smile spread across my twin's face, and he clasped my shoulder. "Congratulations. That is a bond only the Fates could orchestrate, so there is destiny entwined with that declaration."

"Truly," I said, letting the awareness settle into my heart with the love for Gemma and Laurel. "Tomorrow I will rejoice in spilling the blood of the ones who hurt my mates."

A smile spread across Marius's face. I recognized it well as his face of vengeance. "This reminds me of our first battle when Father said never enter a fight that doesn't have importance."

"This is the most important fight I've been in," I said, thinking how I would kiss both my mates until I couldn't hold my faelike form any longer...call them my mates for all to hear. *Erebus, I'll give up my unicorn form to have them with me again.* Then, after they healed, of course, I would show them how much I loved them.

"You should lead us tomorrow. It is your right."

I shook my head. "I prefer to enter under the cover of the distraction. You are our leader. It should always be you."

He nodded. "As you wish. If tomorrow, when we wake, you feel differently, tell me and the helm shall be yours."

"That will not be the case," I said, turning back to the map. Newfound determination blossomed as I thought of having my arms around Gemma and Laurel in less than a day's time. The plan would work, but I wouldn't find rest until my mates were safe. "Besides, I won't be sleeping."

"You should," he said, concern bracketing the corners of his mouth.

"Should and can are two different things," I said.

"I can get you a tonic," he offered.

"No, I don't want to risk it."

"They don't make unicorns groggy if that's what you are worried about."

I turned to face my brother and narrowed my eyes at him. "Why are you so anxious for me to sleep?"

"I'm thinking of your well-being and readiness for tomorrow." False concern permeated his disingenuous tone.

My brother had never questioned my ability before, so why now? Did he think my emotions were too heavily involved? If anything, they only drove me more.

"Shall we take a walk? I could use the night air to center me."

Why was he acting so strangely? I watched Kyle and Jenna for a moment. They were both fast asleep—a deep sleep for vampires.

"Do you not need to check on Arianna?"

"Arianna is with Rainier. I don't think they want to be disturbed."

"Very well." I followed him out of the tent, unable to ignore the twinge of suspicion twisting around my gut. He had referred to his charge as "Arianna" and not "Ari." While that might not have been unusual before the prison kingdom collapsed, he hadn't referred to her as anything but 'Ari' since then.

Marius? I called down our twin bond. He didn't flinch or look my way.

A thunk reverberated in my head. I let my glamour go to my natural form, and the darkness of the night closed in as if there were no moon or stars.

Either he had me blocked out...or this wasn't my brother.

READY FOR MORE? If you haven't read Ari's first book, *Crown of Night and Rain*, start there. Then, read the prequel, *Crown of Broken Promises*, to get caught up on the series. Don't forget Ari's second book arrives this fall!

CRAVING MORE PASSION AND MAGIC?

The magic you've experienced in these pages is just the beginning of the Empire of Curses and Dreams world. Join my newsletter family for exclusive content—from deleted scenes to sneak peeks of upcoming releases. I share writing updates, behind-the-scenes views, and magical surprises with my most devoted readers first. Let's continue this journey together

Acknowledgments

To my friend, Lizzie, thank you for listening when the schedule was crazy (still is), and for making me laugh when I needed it most. Most of all, thanks for sharing experiences in what is otherwise a profession predominantly done in solitude.

To my editors, Dawn and Lisa, this series wouldn't be in existence without the brainstorming, feedback, and encouragement from you. Thank you for pushing me to be a better writer with each book.

To my cover designer, Laura, I am amazed at what you create on our calls every time. You are simply gifted.

To my sister and my nieces, thank you for being there, cheering me on, and listening to me talk about all the aspects of the bookish business. Your support is so meaningful to me!

To my beta readers, ARC readers, and fans, I'm blown away each time you reach out to tell me how much you loved a character. I'm so glad this series has brought us together. Thank you for making me smile and sharing my love of Cyrus!

ABOUT THE AUTHOR

Susan Person is a best-selling and award-winning author of fantasy and dark paranormal romance. After years in the business world, she returned to college to pursue a degree in anthropology and graduated in 2021. Susan enjoys meeting writers and readers alike at conferences and events. She knew at an early age she wanted to write powerful heroines and fulfills that dream by writing badass empowered heroines who take charge in their paranormal worlds.

Susan grew up on a thoroughbred horse farm before moving to the big city of Dallas. She considers herself a Texan but is loyal to her home state of Arkansas. A lover of travel, she has visited several countries with many more to go on her list. She particularly loved dowsing at Stonehenge and seeing the Parthenon in Athens. The outdoors is a place where Susan finds inspiration and can often be found in a park, at the lake, or on a road trip. She especially loves the mountains. Furry animals hold a special place in her heart, and dogs tend to seek her out as a friend.

Connect with her at susanperson.com

WANT TO LEARN MORE ABOUT SUSAN PERSON?

Scan the QR code below to see where you can find more of Susan's book or see what reader events she is attending.

Also by Susan Person

The Night and Rain Series

Crown of Night and Rain, Book 1

Title TBA, Book 2 *(Coming Fall 2025)*

Title To Be Announced, Book 3

Crown of Broken Promises, Prequel

Crown of Ruined Oaths, Book 1.5

The Falling From Hell Series

Fallen, Book 1

Reverie, Book 2

Marred, Book 3

The Blood Moon Prophecy

Queen of Sacrifice, Book 1

Queen of Darkness Book 2

Queen of Moons Book 3

A Vampire Ice Age Series

In Blood & Ice, Book 1

Reclamation In Ice, Book 2

Book 3: TBA

Enchanted Rock Immortals World

Fae Undone, The Enchanted Rock Immortals Clan Fae

Fae Redone, The Enchanted Rock Immortals Clan Fae

www.ingramcontent.com/pod-product-compliance
Lightning Source LLC
Chambersburg PA
CBHW060716190726
48289CB00002B/708